# TRIUMPH OF THE
# DWARF KING

# TRIUMPH OF THE DWARF KING

## THE ADVENTURES OF FINNEGAN DRAGONBENDER™
### BOOK FOUR

CHARLEY CASE    MARTHA CARR    MICHAEL ANDERLE

LMBPN Publishing
PMB 196, 2540 South Maryland Pkwy
Las Vegas, NV 89109

First US edition, February 2020
Version 1.04, July 2021
eBook ISBN: 978-1-64202-732-7
Print ISBN: 978-1-64202-736-5

# DEDICATIONS

### *From Charley*

This book is dedicated to my wife and best friend, Kelly.
Without her belief in my abilities, and patience to see the
process through, this book wouldn't exist.

### *From Martha*

To all those who love to read, and like a good puzzle inside
a good story
To Michael Anderle for his generosity
to all his fellow authors
To Louie and Jackie
And in memory of my big sister,
Dr. Diana Deane Carr
who first taught me about magic, Star Trek,
DC Comics and flaming cherries jubilee

### *From Michael*

To Family, Friends and
Those Who Love
To Read.
May We All Enjoy Grace
To Live The Life We Are
Called.

CHAPTER ONE

Mila sat cross-legged on the hardwood floor beside the dojo mats, her black tank top and leggings soaked with sweat from the intense hour of yoga she had finished. Pulling a hair tie from her wrist, she put her damp hair in a sloppy bun before picking her phone up off the floor. She swigged some water from her Hydro Flask as she hit the button to bring up the web browser.

She typed 'Valkyrie' into the search bar. Scrolling down, she saw the results were an even split between the mythological beings and a movie starring Tom Cruise. Neither was particularly helpful. She settled on a Wikipedia article in her browser history, but it hadn't changed since she read it the day before.

With a sigh, Mila tossed her phone into her lap and leaned back on extended arms. Penny surprised her by coming up from behind and crawling into her lap, picking up her phone, and switching it back on to see what she had been looking at.

The red stripe down the small blue dragon's back

glowed softly in the morning light that streamed through the window. She chuckled at the Wikipedia article.

"Well, it's not like I can get much more information out of you or Finn," Mila said with a wry smile.

Penny tilted her head until they were looking at one another. The dragon's upside-down head smiled. "Shir shee."

In the past few weeks, upon being told she was a Valkyrie, Mila had become more efficient at understanding Penny's half magical language. She still missed a few things here and there, but they could converse with minimal misunderstandings on Mila's part.

Mila smiled back at her friend. "Yeah, I know Valkyries are a rare species, but I feel like if anyone knew anything about them, it would be you two." She raised an eyebrow at Penny. "You two are the only ones on the planet who weren't born here, after all."

Penny looked chagrined. "Chi."

Mila laughed and patted her between the wings. "Don't be sorry. I'm just giving you a hard time. Having someone tell you you're a mythical creature, then in the same breath tell you that they don't know what that means, is a bit of a mixed blessing."

Penny shot a ring of smoke from a nostril in agreement.

Mila settled back onto her arms to watch the action happening on the mats. Finn and Danica had been training hand-to-hand since before sunup. Presently, Finn was using a specialized tool to adjust the dwarven prosthetic attached to Danica's right arm below the elbow.

When Mila had learned that Danica had lost her arm in the battle with the Dark Star's mercenaries, she was livid

Finn hadn't told her right away. She calmed after being told Danica asked him not to tell her anything until the next day. A choice that led to a perfect night for them both.

She smiled, thinking on that first night they had spent together after the soak in the hot tub. They harbored feelings for one another that bordered on fanatic. She just had to break through his walls of self-doubt and the beliefs he had about his past, no small feat, but worth it. She patted herself on the back for that one.

Since then, they hadn't spent a night apart. They had been living an awkward, unfulfilled existence, and now it was as if being together was the norm.

Finn adjusted Danica's prosthetic near the elbow by tightening a dial and looking up at her. "How's that?"

Danica flexed the fingers, bent the wrist, and gave the whole contraption a tug with her other hand. "It's good. I think that dialed it in."

"Good. Let's go through it one more time." He tossed the tool to Mila, who snatched it from the air. "Thanks, babe."

Mila smiled. "No problem, Princeling."

He and Danica both gave her a look like she had just farted from her mouth.

She laughed. "I'm still trying to figure out a good nickname. Don't look at me like that."

"I vote no on princeling," Danica said, then laughed. "It sounds like what you would call a little kid. That's gross."

Mila laughed. "I suppose it does. I'll keep thinking."

"Please do. I don't want to hurl whenever I'm around you two. I like you guys too much." Danica said, settling into a fighting stance.

Mila, for the hundredth time since Hermin had delivered the prosthetic, admired the workmanship of the false limb.

The entire thing looked like a work of art made from twisting strands of a yellowish glass. Finn called it an impact diamond. When Penny did a little digging, she found it was called Lonsdaleite on Earth, and formed when dense graphite meteors impacted the ground. When the celestial body slammed into the Earth, carbon compressed within the meteorite into a compact and robust diamond formation. Finn's people had figured out how to manufacture the stuff without the flaws that naturally formed from impact and used it in applications where strength was vital. Mila had laughed at the idea that Danica's new arm was priceless, yet worthless in any practical application. It turned out that Lonsdaleite was so rare humanity didn't have a use for it beyond it being a marker of a meteor impact site.

The twisting strands of the prosthetic danced in an intricate weave over and under themselves, leaving diamond-shaped holes all along the appendage until it reached the intricate wrist that could move in an even better arc than a human wrist. The palm and back of the hand were formed with more of the intricate design and ended in fingers made of delicate cylinders formed into long digits that matched Danica's other hand once Finn adjusted their size and length.

The prosthetic's connection to her arm was magical, and the only real downside. It had taken Danica a few days to get used to channeling magic into the device to get it to move naturally. She didn't need to control it with magic,

that was done through some mental connection that mimicked the natural movement, but it was a constant if small drain on her magic.

However, the upside was that her hand was now stronger than any natural appendage had a right to be. On the second day, Danica accidentally crushed a pair of metal *Baoding* therapy balls she was using to hone her fine motor skills. She had the steel balls in her hand, rotating them with her fingers like she was supposed to be when Mila had dropped a glass, Danica started and reacted by crunching the balls into a single deformed mass. Since then, she took care not to accidentally crush herself or anyone else.

Finn and Danica lined up, settling into their preferred stances.

"Ready?" Finn asked.

In answer, Danica came at him, shuffling in low, her long legs bending at the knee and bare feet moving quickly. She sent a lightning jab with her left arm at his stomach, yet Finn sidestepped. She followed with an uppercut with her right, making Finn lean his head back. Danica's diamond-hard fist brushed his beard but missed his chin by three inches.

Finn reached out and grabbed the wrist of her left hand as she pulled it back, pulling her off balance. He continued the pull and spun her around to grab her from behind in a bear hug, but Danica saw the move coming and dropped to the ground, pulling him forward and forcing him to bend at the waist. She bunched up her long legs and kicked upward, hitting him in the chest and knocking him off his feet, and over top of her in a flip.

Finn, instead of letting go of her wrist, clamped down even harder and twisted as he went over the top, making Danica have to roll or have her wrist broken.

The elf ended up on her stomach, her arm twisted behind her, and pinned under Finn's knee.

He smiled. "Well done, Danica. Good use of your new abilities."

Mila was confused. It looked like Finn had dominated the entire encounter, but he was congratulating her.

"What did she do? It looked like she lost to me." Mila said, sitting up straighter to get a better look.

Finn released Danica's arm and stood. Danica rolled to the side, revealing that when Finn had landed, she had gripped her prosthetic hand around his ankle.

Finn grinned. "In a real fight, she could have crushed my ankle, and I would have been out of it." He reached down and helped the tall elf to her feet. "Now you're starting to think like you have an enhancement instead of a disability. Keep it up, and I'll be afraid to spar with you soon."

She beamed. "Thanks. You were right. This thing is better than I dreamed. With a good concealment spell, I'll be able to go back to work, and no one will know anything had happened." She flexed the Lonsdalleite fingers. "It feels like a normal hand, as far as touch. I can't feel temperature though. It's a little discomfiting, but I can live with it."

Finn nodded. "Yeah, we never figured out temperature. I'm glad it's working out for you, though."

Mila tapped Penny on the shoulder. "I'm getting up." Penny scurried up onto her shoulder, and Mila got to her feet, feeling the sore muscles from her yoga session. She let

out a small grunt. Brushing off the seat of her pants, she asked, "You guys want some breakfast?"

"You don't need to ask me twice," Finn said.

"I'm famished," Danica added.

"Shir!" Penny grinned and patted Mila on the top of her head. She laughed at the dragon and went to the kitchen to cook eggs and sausage.

It had been two weeks since the events at Grand Lake. They had stayed at Preston's cabin for another week in the protective cover of the wards in case the Dark Star, Hellena, stuck around to exact revenge right away. They had spent the days as a vacation, for once not having to look over their shoulders for assassins and hitmen trying to cash in on the outrageous bounties Hellena had put on their heads. Hermin had returned with the prosthetic two days later and told them that there was no sign of the Dark Star or her men in the area, and the Huldu were keeping a close eye on the situation.

When they returned home, they found Remmy and her tribe had abided by the rules Finn and Mila had laid out, perhaps a little too precisely. They had come into the condo to find thirty naked and showered goblins. They were clean as thirty whistles, and the furniture and other items in the home were spotless, pots and pans washed and stored; however, it was a lot of little green butts to lay eyes on.

The tribe's leader, an elderly goblin named Redik, who thanked them for the time they had at the condo, had said if they ever needed anything, to feel free and ask. His people would do their best to return the favor.

Grace had gotten a hold of them two days after Finn's

initial request to buy the condo building and told him she could set up a purchase price of just over ten million dollars. That price included the signed documentation of all the tenants who agreed to sell at an inflated market rate. Finn concurred, and Mila transferred the money to an escrow account, pending all the paperwork, which they signed digitally while at the cabin. They expected the sale to finalize anytime.

Mila was excited to convert it into communal housing for those that needed it in the magical community. Even if he didn't know it, Finn was gathering a loyal following from those who were often overlooked.

Mila turned and smiled at the sight of Finn, showing Danica another set of moves, and her friend engaged in the exchange. She had worried that Danica would suffer side effects from the loss of her arm, and she had moments, but overall, Danica displayed an impressive amount of tenacity to make Mila proud of her friend.

Mila loaded the plates and poured cups of coffee, dropping a few Charleston Chews into Penny's and Finn's. They sat down and tore into the food, their workouts demanding calories.

After eating, as Mila was loading the dishwasher, Finn broke the silence. "We need to find Hellena." He leaned back in his chair, a frown on his face. "Preston says her followers are increasing activities, and he's having trouble keeping them covered up with his G.A.E.L. forces."

Mila put the last plate in the washer and leaned on the counter. She grabbed her coffee while saying, "You want to hunt her down? I thought we were laying low a few more days."

Finn gave her a half-smile. "Things are moving too fast for us to take more time off. You hurt her badly at the lake, your celestial magic didn't interact well with her dark magic. Chances are she's still nursing her wounds. At least in the short term. If we can find her now, then we choose the battlefield, and she won't be at full strength." He grimaced. "At least that's the hope."

"So, where do we start?" Danica asked.

Finn shook his head. "You start by getting back to a normal life. I don't want you getting hurt again."

Danica gave him a sour look. "I don't think you get to decide that for me, big guy. I've made sacrifices for this fight, and I don't regret any of it."

Mila smiled at her friend's fire but understood what Finn was saying. "Danica, I know you're a bad-ass and a great ally, but right now, we don't even know where Hellena is. You have patients waiting for you to come back. Plus, I overheard you talking to Phil on the phone." Mila smiled. "I bet he's busting to see you again."

Danica frowned but nodded. "I suppose you're right, but you tell me the minute you know where she is. Don't leave me out of this." She held up her prosthetic so everyone could see it. "I owe her one."

Finn took a sip of coffee. "You'll know when we know. Promise."

"So...where do we begin?" Mila asked.

Finn blew out a long breath. "No idea."

# CHAPTER TWO

A popping sound made Finn jump to his feet, his coffee sloshing onto the table. He reached for Fragar and cursed when he realized he wasn't wearing his harness.

"Hello, all. Sorry to drop in unannounced."

Finn relaxed when he saw that it was Garret and Hermin in their usual stained overalls. Garret gave them a wave.

"Hey, boys." Danica waved, chuckling at Finn's over-reaction.

The two Huldu stopped short. Hermin gave Danica a once over. "I'll have you know, young lady, we are well older than 'boys.'"

Garret joined in. "We were there when Rome fell. Can you say that? Show some respect to your elders."

Danica held her hands up. "Whoa. I didn't mean any disrespect. It's a figure of speech. You both have such… youthful complexions."

Finn raised an eyebrow at the two old gnomes. They

were anything but youthful, but they ate her compliment up.

"Oh, well, then." Garret beamed, standing straighter. "You should know Hermin is a hundred years older than me."

This got a laugh from everyone, and Finn indicated they should sit at the table with them. "Would you two like a cup of coffee?"

"Oh, that would be marvelous," Garret said, sitting down beside Danica.

"Could you put some of those little candies in it, the way you like it, Finn?" Hermin added.

Finn smiled, going over to fetch two mugs. "I knew you were my favorite, Hermin."

Once everyone had their mugs and were settled, Finn asked, "What can we do for you two?"

The Huldu glanced at one another. "Well, it may be nothing," Hermin said, "but we thought it might be of interest to you. Ever since Grand Lake, we have been making efforts to find the Dark Star through a tracking spell."

Garret picked up where Hermin left off, the way only two people who have worked together for a thousand years could. "Normally, a tracking spell needs a name and some basic information about the object. Right now, we only know her first name and not much else. She is blocking our attempts, but that takes energy, and we figured she'll slip up eventually."

"But she hasn't." Hermin continued. "We can still lock on places she's been in the past."

Garret added, "Sometimes."

Hermin nodded. "Sometimes. We think." He mysteriously waved a hand. "It's not an exact science. However, we have gotten multiple hits in Boulder." He gave them a knowing look.

Finn frowned and looked around the table, the slightly confused looks from the others let him know he wasn't the only one confused.

"You're saying she might be in Boulder?" Finn asked slowly.

The two Huldu rolled their eyes.

"No," Garret said with forced patience. "We went to Boulder and looked. She's not there. We're just saying it's odd that it keeps popping up. When a tracking spell doesn't work, you usually get a flurry of places, some stronger than others — that's how we can tell if it's a place she has been — but mostly it's just random locations. For it to pop up in a place twice is rare, but for it to keep happening is something else. We just don't know what."

Finn saw that Penny had a contemplative look on her face, tapping at her chin with a talon. "You have an idea?"

Penny shrugged. "Shiri, chi shee?"

Finn raised an eyebrow. "Would that be possible? Could it be a relative of hers?"

Garret thought it over. "It's possible. It would have to be someone closely related. A sibling or a parent, maybe. But we don't know anything but her first name. How would we know who it is?"

Finn sighed and finished his coffee. He set the mug down, thinking things through. "I don't know if this information will help, but it can't hurt, I suppose. I have someone I need to talk to that might help. Preston might be able to do something with the Boulder angle, have you talked to him about it?"

Hermin nodded. "I spoke with him just before coming here. He said he would investigate. Who are you going to speak with?"

"Gwen," Finn said, standing and going to the coat rack where his harness was hanging and put it on.

Garret raised an eyebrow. "The dryad? How could she help? Doesn't she run a food cart?"

Finn smiled. "Yeah, but she hears a lot, and we have a pretty good relationship. You want to come Mila? You can try a tooter."

Mila shrugged. "Sure. Let me get a quick shower and change, though."

He nodded, going back to the coffee pot and grumbling when he saw it was empty. "No problem. I need to make more coffee anyway."

---

Finn and Mila stepped off the magical staircase that led from the alley and into the bustling underground Market. Penny was riding Finn's shoulder, but as soon as they were in the vaulted chamber, she gave a "Chi, chi!" of explanation and flew ahead of them to get a few tooters in before they arrived.

"She really loves tooters, huh?" Mila smiled after the small dragon as she shot over the various tents towards the center of the Market.

Finn laughed. "Well, they are a tasty treat. A bit like

maple sausage and the white stuff in an Oreo wrapped in flaky pastry."

Mila gave him a confused look as they fell into the flow of foot traffic. "I thought you said it was grilled meat."

"It is." Finn nodded and smiled. "Not all meat comes from a cow or a pig, you know."

She smacked his arm. "I can't help that I grew up without knowing better."

"I've seen you refuse lamb because they're too cute to eat."

"That's different," she said haughtily. "I stand by the idea that you shouldn't eat cute things." She frowned. "Tooters aren't cute, are they?"

Finn laughed. "Not even a little bit. Vicious little bastards if they ever go wild. For a long time, they were treated as vermin, and exterminated throughout the galaxy, until some desperate fool ate one. Then they were considered a delicacy and raised in farms."

They meandered through the stalls, stopping when something caught their eye. Finn enjoyed talking with Mila. She was more knowledgeable than most people. She rattled off facts about the strangest things, yet always made Finn think she was happy he was in on it, unlike people who used their knowledge to make themselves feel superior.

Mila paused at a stall and held a small medallion up to get a look. Her face split into a smile. "Check this out. It's a Roman coin. This is the face of Augustus. He rebuilt the Roman Empire after his uncle Julius Caesar was killed. A pretty important guy as far as history is concerned."

She asked the man behind the counter how much, and

he quoted a price, and she began haggling. Finn smiled when she began using her knowledge of ancient artifacts to point out that Roman coins were not all that rare, and she would be willing to pay the going rate, pulling out her phone and finding several similar coins for half the price he quoted. The stall owner relented and sold it to her at a fair price. She then slipped him an extra hundred and thanked him for the lively bartering.

She held the coin, looking at the preserved detail in it as they headed for Gwen's stall.

"You really love old things, don't you?" Finn asked, making her look up and redden a little.

"Well, yeah." She held up the coin. "Think of all the people who treasured this over the last two thousand years. The goods that were bought with it. This coin was minted in Rome sometime around year one, and somehow it ended up in a magical market under Denver. That's incredible."

Finn nodded, appreciating the coin more. "While that is pretty interesting, why did you buy it?"

She smiled and handed the coin to him. "Augustus was known for a few things, but the major two were that during his reign, his people experienced peace from large-scale conflict for the first time in a long time, and also he expanded the Roman Empire halfway around the world."

Finn took the coin, hefting its weight in his hand.

"I thought you might like to keep it as a reminder," she said.

Finn frowned. "A reminder of what?"

"A reminder that as a prince, your job is to bring peace

to your people and provide for them what you can," she said.

Finn raised an eyebrow. "But I don't have a people. I'm an exile."

She smiled and waved a hand around the chamber filled with magicals going about their business. "These are your people. They may not swear fealty to you, but they need your help, even if they don't know it. You already started taking care of them when you bought our building and plan on letting magicals stay there as a sanctuary because they have nowhere else to go."

"That's just doing the right thing. It doesn't make me their prince."

"You have the means and the will. That's more than most people ever get from their leaders. There will always be people like the Dark Star, trying to take what they want or force people to bend to their will, and there will always be people like you who oppose them and seek nothing in return." She leaned into him as they walked and wrapped both her arms around his sizeable right arm, hugging it tightly. "That's one of the things I love most about you. You give a shit."

They arrived at the food court in the middle of the Market. People ate food from the various food carts that lined the area, many standing, some sitting at multiple picnic tables. Finn spotted Penny and Gwen the Dryad chatting at her cart, the Dryad throwing her head back and laughing, her large tongs holding a blue-glazed tooter above a paper boat...which Penny was lying in. The dragon's outstretched hands and her frustration at the out-of-reach tooter made Finn laugh.

Gwen lowered the tongs so Penny could grab the sweetmeat. "Sorry, darlin', but that joke was too much for my old roots. You shoulda waited till I handed ye the fookin' thing." She saw Finn approaching with Mila on his arm. "Finn! Bout time you got yer sorry ass over here. Penny's eating me out of house and fookin' home."

"We were looking at the stalls," he said, slipping the Augustus coin into his pocket.

She gave Mila an appraising look. "Just lookin', huh? Poor girl." She winked at Mila, making her blush.

Gwen held out a small hand and smiled, her pointed teeth making Mila do a double-take. "You must be Mila. Finn has been hemm'n and haw'n o'er ye fer as long as I've known 'em. Good to see he took me advisement. Tooter?" she clacked her tongs, making Mila jump.

"That would be wonderful."

The small woman pulled two of the blue treats off the grill and dropped them into paper boats, while Penny chomped down the last bite of hers and watched the boats pass over her.

"Thanks, Gwen," Finn said, taking the boat and inhaling the sweet smell. "I came to see if you've heard anything from your tree recently."

Gwen raised an eyebrow, her hands on her hips. "I hear from her every day, ye daft fooker. I'm a fookin' Dryad."

Finn chuckled. "I understand that, I was speaking of the corruption it had pointed out a few weeks ago. Anything like that?"

Gwen narrowed her eyes. "Goin' after her, are ya? Well, I can't say I don't blame you. Someone needs to take care o' her, and the Earth knows it ain't goin' to be those useless

Huldu. Barely keep the place runnin' as it is without havin' ta fight off the random world-dominatin' megalomaniac." She huffed, blowing a strand of hair out of her large eyes. "But, no. My tree's been quiet on that front. Why?"

"We can't find her. We know she's hurt, but no one can get a bead on her."

Gwen considered, clacking the tongs a few times. "I dunno what to tell ye, big feller. Could probably ask the Dirt Elemental. If you can find 'em, anyway."

Finn frowned. "The Dirt Elemental?"

She nodded. "Big bastard made of dirt and shit. The elemental's kinda like a..." she weighed her words, "a titan for Earth. Or, I guess you could call him the Earth's hands. The problem is he kinda does whatever he wants, but if the shit really hits the fan, he might show up."

"How do I contact him?" Finn asked, hearing a crunch and looking over to see a surprised look on Mila's face as she bit into the crispy larvae.

"Iss is amazing!" she said around a mouth full of sweetmeat.

"Told you. These things are a delicacy. And Gwen here makes the best," Finn said, with a sly look Gwen's way.

Gwen smacked him with the tongs. "Don't ye be tryin' to butter me up. Besides, I don't know how to contact him. No one does. He sorta shows up. And don't go askin' around, not many people e'en know about him. It's a bit of a secret if ye know what I mean."

Finn had no idea what she meant, but he nodded.

Mila held up a chunk of meat. "What part of the tooter is this?"

Gwen raised an eyebrow. "It's the whole thing."

Mila cocked her head at Finn. "I thought you said they were some kind of varmint."

"Yeah." Finn took a big bite of his and continued with his mouth full. "Unce eh eu-pate."

"Pupate?" She looked at the blue thing in her hands with a closer eye. "This is a larva?" Her face turned slightly green.

"Ye wouldn't wanna eat 'em once they're adults, dearie. Poison taints the meat."

"P...Poison?" Mila rushed to the closest trashcan and lost her lunch along with her breakfast, and maybe even a little of the previous night's dinner.

"Kids these days," Gwen said, shaking her head.

Penny let out a huff of flaming disappointment when she saw Mila had wasted a perfectly good tooter.

## CHAPTER THREE

F inn followed Mila and Danica as they walked arm-in-arm down the sidewalk, huddled together for warmth, and whispering to one another. They had dressed for a night out, Danica taking special care to pick something that would show off her arm so she could practice her concealment spell in public before returning to work the next day.

Mila went with black ankle boots and leggings under a dark blue skater dress and her waist-length leather jacket for a bit of warmth in the chilly winter air. Danica wore black ankle boots and leggings, and her red dress came to a halter neck, exposing her shoulders and arms; although, on the way to the Refinery, she wore a thick and fluffy white poncho.

Penny was snuggled in her hammock, attached to the back of Finn's harness, hidden under his bomber jacket, playing a game on Finn's phone. He could hear her growling as the game got the better of her.

Finn took a few quick steps, going up the short

stairway ahead of the ladies so he could open the door for them. "After you," he said with a smile.

"Such a gentleman." Danica teased, stepping to the warm and lively bar. Finn followed, and the sound of live folk music and conversation hit him with a warm, familiar feeling.

Danny, the Scottish born bartender, was behind the bar, slinging drinks to a full house. He gave them a friendly wave when he spotted his regulars and signaled he'd pour them their regular beverages in a few minutes. Finn gave a nod of thanks and followed Danica as she searched for an open table.

Danica led the way to a high table that opened up after a few seconds, and they claimed the limited seating. Danica and Mila hung their jacket and poncho on the hooks attached to the underside of the table then settled onto the high stools. Finn pulled the small service animal vest out and handed it to Penny when she climbed out of his jacket.

The small dragon rolled her eyes but slipped the vest on before grabbing a handful of peanuts the previous patrons left on the table.

"I'll take these up," Mila said, gathering some empty glassware. "Does anyone want anything other than the usual?"

"Chi! Shiri chi." Penny said around a mouthful of peanuts.

Mila raised an eyebrow. "An old fashioned? Really? Okay, you got it. Anyone else?"

Finn shook his head. "I'm good with a beer and whiskey."

Mila laughed. "So, the usual?"

He chuckled. "Yeah, I guess so."

"I'm good with a G&T. Though if you could grab another old fashioned, that would be great." Danica smiled and turned a little red. "Phil really likes them."

Mila, Finn, and Penny all gave her a look.

"I invited him," she confessed. "We haven't seen each other in two weeks, and I wanted to see if he noticed the arm." She held up the prosthetic, looking like her natural skin, with the concealment spell wrapped around it. "I know the spell will fool people, but I have to make sure he can't feel it."

"The spell will do the work," Finn assured her, reaching out and taking the artificial hand in his. When he concentrated, he could feel the elaborate material but only because he knew what to look for. To anyone else, it would feel like skin, maybe a little on the solid side, but the spell would coax their mind into feeling what they expected.

Danica gave a smile and nodded. "I have to admit, I'm a little nervous. And to that end, I'm going to go pee before he gets here." She hopped off her stool and headed for the back.

Mila leaned in and gave Finn a quick kiss. "That was nice of you, reassuring her."

He smiled at the attention. "I was stating the facts. Danica will be fine. Especially when we get a gin and tonic in her. Besides, when you come up against trouble, it's never half as bad if you face up to it."

Mila laughed. "That's wisdom."

"That's who Danica is," he said, watching the tall elf weave her way through the crowd. "She doesn't turn from a challenge. She'll be alright."

Mila nodded in agreement, watching Danica go as well. "I'll be back with the drinks. You stay here and watch the table."

Finn and Penny sat and watched the local band on stage while they waited. It was a duo act, the guy playing the violin and the girl an acoustic guitar and singing. The song was good, something about finding love while running from the devil, but the melody was catchy, and their musical talents really shined.

"I always like live music, man," a deep voice rumbled.

Finn hopped off his stool, and Penny was on his shoulder in an instant, inflating with dragon fire.

Rolf was in Danica's stool, drinking seltzer water. "Sorry. Didn't mean to scare you." The old stoner gave them a big-eyed smile.

Finn relaxed. "Rolf. How the hell do you do that?"

"Do what?" he asked, reaching out and snagging a few peanuts and tossing them in his mouth.

Penny was so shocked, she didn't even protest.

"You just pop up out of nowhere. Is it magic?" Finn frowned.

Rolf laughed. "No, man. I'm just quiet." He gave Penny a wave. "You must be Penny. I'm Rolf. It's nice to meet you."

Penny gave him a hesitant wave, and Finn felt her relax on his shoulder. She climbed down to the table and slid the bowl of peanuts to the other side of the table, out of Rolf's reach. She tossed one in her mouth and crunched it up, watching the old soldier as he unraveled his long red scarf.

"So how did it go fighting that crazy witch?" Rolf asked, pursing his lips and settling on one of his elbows.

"How did..." Finn shook his head, "doesn't matter. It

went okay, I suppose. I was able to use my magic while in a rage."

Rolf's eyes widened. "Really? So soon?" He huffed. "Took me a good year of practice to do it the first time, man. I can't believe you bust it out in a few days."

"Well, I had a tenuous grasp on the magic at best, but I was able to cast a few spells," Finn admitted. "I really need to ramp up the abilities if I'm going to be fighting people on the Dark Star's level. Do you have any new steps for me?"

Rolf sucked at his teeth then took a long drink of seltzer. "Yeah, there is, but to be honest, you need to keep going with the breathing and mantra. Those two things are a foundation for the rest of the techniques. You might be able to cast, but as you said, it was tenuous at best. You don't want to build a house on sand, man, you need a good solid foundation to build that place. When you can cast without trouble during a rage, we can move on."

"Really? Just keep on keeping on?" Finn asked. "Is that why you showed up? To tell me to not do anything differently?"

Rolf laughed. "Be pretty funny if I did." When Finn gave him a furrowed brow, Rolf continued, "Actually, I have a favor to ask you."

"Okay. I do owe you. What can I do?"

Rolf squinted one eye and readjusted himself in on the stool, putting his thoughts together. "I'm not exactly sure, to tell the truth, but I figured you were the best shot at an answer." He looked from Finn to Penny and back. "Have either of you noticed magic acting up?"

Finn frowned. "Acting up? Like how?"

"Well, like when you cast a spell it tries to, like, I don't know, man...like it tries to do something else. Just a little. It's subtle, but I think its getting worse." Rolf seemed uncomfortable thinking about it, rubbing at the back of his neck and grimacing.

Finn shook his head and opened his mouth, but Penny spoke first.

"Shiri squee. Chi chi shir." Her eye ridges furrowed as she looked up at Finn.

"Really? You noticed it too? Why didn't you say anything?" Finn asked, surprised. He hadn't felt any change whatsoever. Then again, he tended to use magic more like a hammer than a delicate tool the way Penny did.

She shrugged. "Shir?"

"What did she say?" Rolf asked, leaning in.

"She said it only happened a couple of times, and it was so subtle she didn't think much of it, blaming it on a lack of concentration," Finn translated.

Rolf looked confused, glancing from Finn to Penny. "You got all of that from one word?"

Finn chuckled. "Dragon language is not like natural languages. It's magical, the sounds having a slight impact on what is being said."

"Far out, man," Rolf said, a new appreciation for the small dragon on his face.

"Why do you think I could help with this, though?" Finn was still unsure what Rolf was asking of him.

Rolf sat back and shrugged. "Because you fix all sorts of weird shit. Plus, it started a few days after you put the beat down on the Dark Star."

"You think it's connected to her?"

"Probably, man. That woman has been fuckin shit up all over the place for a while now. I wouldn't put it past her to try and fuck up magic too." Rolf gave a lazy shrug. "That woman is insane. Dark magic makes people do weird shit."

"I still don't really see how I can help."

Rolf finished off his seltzer. "I was hoping you could ask your Huldu friends. They seem to know what's up most of the time."

Finn cocked his head and regarded Rolf. "Can't you ask them?"

"Me and the gnomes...well, let's say we don't get along too well." He looked past Finn and pointed. "You should probably help her."

Finn turned and saw Mila struggling to get all the drinks off the bar. Finn hopped off the stool and, in two long steps, was at her side.

"Let me get some of these." He said, picking up four of the drinks in his large hands.

"Thanks." Mila grabbed the bottle of beer and her drink along with a fresh bowl of peanuts.

They turned back, and Finn leaned in to be heard over the music. "There's someone I want you..." he trailed off when he saw Penny sitting at the table alone watching them. She saw his look and turned around, seeming surprised that Rolf was gone as well.

"What?" Mila asked, leaning in to hear better.

"Never mind," Finn said, rolling his eyes.

# CHAPTER FOUR

F inn and Mila arrived at the table at the same time as Danica, but when Finn set down the drinks, Danica passed them by, heading for the door.

"Hey, your drink is over here," Finn said to the elf's retreating back, then he saw what had grabbed her attention.

Phil, the lanky, odd man from the morgue they had met a while back, had come in the door and was looking around nervously as he removed a thick yellow scarf. When he laid eyes on Danica, he brightened and moved to meet her, waving a floppy hand at her while grinning ear to ear.

"Huh," Mila grunted, climbing onto her stool and watching the odd man. "He's more handsome than I remember."

"Probably the fact that he's not being washed out by fluorescent lights," Finn said, then added, "And not surrounded by dead bodies."

She gave Finn a sly grin. "I don't know. You're still handsome when surrounded by dead bodies."

Finn snorted a laugh, then his jaw dropped when he saw Danica wrap her arms around Phil's neck and kiss him passionately. Even Phil seemed taken aback by her aggressive manner.

"Did you know about that?" Finn asked, turning to the table and getting rolled eyes from both Penny and Mila. "So just me then?"

"Just you." Mila patted his hand.

Finn sat, then stood again when Danica and Phil approached. Finn extended a steady hand. "Phil. Good to see you again."

Phil shook the offered hand, his shoulders bouncing when Finn pumped their arms up and down vigorously. "Good to see you too, Finn. Mila, how are you?"

"I'm pretty goo—"

"Holy shit!" Phil shouted, jumping back from the table and pointing. "There's a lizard in the peanuts!"

"That's just Penny," Danica assured him. "She's a, uh, pet?"

Penny gave her a hard stare before tossing a peanut into her mouth and chewing it while keeping eye contact.

"More like a friend, really," Danica amended, giving Penny an apologetic shrug.

"Sit," Finn decided they should move on before Penny said something she would regret, "Danica got you an old fashioned. How are things at the morgue? Business been lively?"

Everyone groaned at the pathetic joke until they saw

the confused look on Finn's face. "What's so funny?" Then everyone laughed for real.

Mila took pity on him and explained the 'lively' joke.

"Oh, right. Puns, or whatever. I don't really do that."

Mila chuckled. "Not on purpose, anyway."

Finn rolled his eyes, bringing on more laughter.

Phil judiciously approached the table, his stare locked on Penny. The tiny dragon gave him a grin, and he flinched. "I don't think I've ever seen anything like her."

"I got her on a trip to…" Finn wasn't good enough with Earth geography to come up with something off the top of his head.

Mila, however, was. "Peru. He found her in darkest Peru."

Phil laughed.

"What's so funny?" Mila asked.

"Darkest Peru?" Phil asked. "Like Paddington Bear?"

Mila's face turned red. "Yup. Just like Paddington Bear."

Phil stuck a finger out to presumably scratch Penny's chin, but a quick clack of teeth from her made him think better. "She's a sweetheart, isn't she?"

Mila chuckled. "Actually, she's kind of an asshole."

Penny gave her an aggrieved look.

"But, she's our asshole, and we love her."

Penny relaxed in the bowl of nuts and puffed out a smoke ring of agreement.

"Is that smoke?" Phil said wide-eyed.

Finn, thinking fast, scooted Phil's drink closer to him. "So, you're Danica's boyfriend now?"

Danica, who happened to be taking a sip, snorted and shot G&T from her nose.

Phil quickly found her some napkins and helped her clean up.

Mila leaned in and whispered to Finn. "Way to be subtle, knuckles." She winced. "Never mind the knuckles part. I don't know why I thought that would work as a nickname."

Finn chuckled at her horrible choice of pet name for him. "It may not have been subtle, but he stopped asking questions about Penny."

For the next couple of hours, they all chatted and enjoyed the music. Danica and Phil kept their canoodling to a minimum, but it was still a little uncomfortable when they would have their heads close together, whispering god knew what to one another.

Finn did notice that Danica kept her prosthetic away from Phil for the most part, not letting his finger linger on it for more than a second. Despite her desire to be close, she was wary.

Finn drained his beer and thought about his conversation with Rolf. If magic was twisting, then something was doing the twisting. His money was on the Dark Star. Hellena was a magic-user and a potent one at that, so messing with magic seemed like it would hurt her more than help.

Finn's eyes widened. "What if she's trying to trigger peabrains into waking up?"

The conversation at the table stopped. Everyone looked at the dwarf as if he had sprouted an arm from his forehead. He glanced at their reactions, realizing he had said that out loud.

"Sorry, thinking about the Dark...uh, Hellena." He gave Phil, the only unawakened person there a sidelong glance. "Hey, Phil, would you mind getting another round? Just have Danny put it on my tab."

"Uh, sure." Phil got up, collected the empty glasses, and headed for the bar.

Danica leaned in, her brow furrowed in anger. "What the hell, Finn? He's going to think you don't like him."

"Sorry." Finn smiled apologetically. "I had a thought, but first, have you noticed your magic acting funny?"

Danica raised an eyebrow. "Funny how?"

"Chir shee," Penny said, having been the only other person who had been present for Rolf's talk.

"Yeah, like it's fighting you. Trying to do something else," Finn said, nodding to Penny.

Danica thought about it. "I mean, it's been a little sluggish lately, but I figured it was from me having to power this all the time." She held up the artificial hand.

"What's going on?" Mila cut in, not having any clue where any of this was coming from.

"Rolf stopped by and asked us to look into something. He said magic has been acting weird for him, and it started a few days after we fought Hellena at the lake." Finn pointed to Penny. "She said she noticed it a few times, but it wasn't anything she was alarmed about. As far as I can tell, from what they are saying, magic still works, but it's like listening to a radio slightly out of tune."

"What does that have to do with triggering peabrains?" Mila asked.

"I was trying to think of why she would do something

that would mess with her own power. Sometimes, if there is a big release of magic, or something happens to destabilize it, it can, in theory, wake people up that don't know they are magical. Maybe she's trying to force magic out into the open by waking a bunch of people. Like enough of them, the Huldu can't cover it up."

"Like how many people?" Mila asked.

Finn shrugged and looked at Penny, who gave a shrug as well. "A couple hundred? The whole city? I don't know."

Danica blinked a few times, trying to imagine the whole city waking up at once. "That would be a disaster. It would change the world as we know it. I mean, governments aren't trustworthy as it is, but you show them a whole city of magical beings, and I'm pretty sure most of us would disappear overnight, locked up in some lab somewhere."

Finn saw the look of horror on her face. "Well, it's just a theory. If that's what she's doing, she'd have to ramp up the power. As it stands, I didn't even notice it was happening. If I had to guess, we have some time before peabrains start randomly waking. But, that means we really need to find her, and soon."

Phil returned with a tray full of drinks, and everyone leaned back from the huddle they had formed while talking.

"Did I miss anything?" he asked, passing out drinks.

"Nothing important," Danica assured him, smiling and taking the drink he offered.

Phil smiled back and held up the tray. "Be right back." He turned and jogged off to return the tray to the bar.

Danica's sweet smile fell, and she gave Finn a hard look.

"You need to find that crazy bitch, and end this. I don't want to have to go hunting for another boyfriend because this one is locked up in some government lab."

Finn smiled. "So he *is* your boyfriend."

Penny, Mila, and Danica all groaned.

# CHAPTER FIVE

Finn, Mila, and Penny decided to leave Danica and Phil alone and headed home early. On the walk, Mila held onto his arm, and hummed a nameless tune, a smile on her face as she kept her thoughts to herself, and Penny curled around her neck like a scarf.

Finn was happy. It had been a long time since he could say it. Sure, an insane woman was trying to rip the world apart, and Finn was the tip of the spear to stop her, but it was another thing on his to-do list. He had come here to find treasure and wealth, and instead found something far more valuable.

This old ship he walked on had become so much more than its creators intended. It was now his home. A warm beacon in the galaxy where the races lived together. Well, maybe not together, exactly, but pretty close.

Finn frowned. That was what bothered him most about Hellena. She saw the same thing he did, the inequality and willingness to overlook those who were not the norm to keep up the facade of a nonmagical world. He wanted to do something about that inequality, but he didn't know what. Hellena, on the other hand, had made a plan and was enacting it. He gave her credit for that.

Hellena's plan was horrible and would cost millions, if not billions of lives, but at least she was doing something.

"What's wrong?" Mila asked, feeling his change in mood.

Finn frowned. "Are we doing the right thing?"

Mila's brows rose. "About the Dark Star? Yes. We are absolutely doing the right thing. If she has her way, the world will be at war. Trust me, we don't need another one of those. What made you ask that?"

Finn shook his head. "I don't know. I guess when you really think about it, she and I want the same thing, the only difference is that I have no idea how to make it happen. Her plan is bad and will cost a lot of lives, but it will get the job done in the end."

Mila stopped and turned to face him. "That's not true."

"I'm pretty sure that if a magical army tries to take enough land to build a nation, then magicals will be out in the open no matter how much anyone tries to cover it up," Finn said with a sad grin.

"No, I mean the part where you and she want the same things. Hellena wants magicals to be in the open with a nation of their own. She wants to be able to use political power to shape the world. She wants to be in control. You don't want any of those things." Mila put a small hand on his chest. "You want people to have a better life. You want them to have a chance to move ahead in the world. You don't want power or influence, you just want people to be safe and happy. It's what makes you a leader, despite not wanting to lead. Maybe you two started out with the same desires, but her dark magic has twisted her."

"That doesn't mean she's wrong about magicals not needing to hide. They should be free to be themselves," Finn said.

Mila sighed. "Sometimes being right and doing the right thing isn't compatible."

Finn thought on that, then nodded. "The greater good argument."

Mila shook her head. "No. The least harm argument. Neither one of us knows why the magicals went into hiding when the peabrains lost magic, but I have to believe it was for a good reason. We can't let Hellena make the decision to expose them without knowing the whole truth."

"You're right." Finn agreed, taking her hand and continuing towards the condo. "We will stop her. Then we can look into how to help those who need it." He was silent for a few steps. "Speaking of helping those who need it, have you thought about asking your old professor Hoffensteffer if he knows anything about Valkyries?"

Mila peered at him in confusion. "Why would he know anything?"

Finn shrugged. "I don't know. He studies history and is in the know about magic. I figured it was a good place to start."

Mila stopped in her tracks. "I forgot about him knowing about magic. I think of him as the doddering old man that taught me to love history."

Finn glanced to see if she was joking. "You cut a Kashgar's hand off in his office. How did you forget about that?"

Mila snorted. "Oh, yeah. That was my first hand-chop."

Finn chuckled. "Good times."

"I'll send him a text," she said, pulling out her phone.

They had walked another block by the time she hit the send button. "There, that should give him a nice shock."

"What did you say?"

Mila shrugged. "The truth. I'm a Valkyrie, and I don't know what that means, and if he knows anything, he should give me a call." Her eyes twinkled with mischief. "The mystery will drive him nuts."

"How long—" Finn started, but was cut off when her phone *dinged*.

She looked at the screen. "Well, that was fast." She read the reply, and her eyes went wide. "Holy shit. He says he's on his way."

Finn, remembering their flight to Toronto, did a little quick math. "Well, it's only seven, and the flight we took was..." he trailed off, counting the hours on his fingers, "so he should be here sometime in the morning, assuming he leaves for the airport right now."

Mila shook her head. "He sent a second message. He says he'll be here in twenty minutes."

Finn raised an eyebrow. "Well, I guess he knows some people who can teleport. Makes sense. Come on, we need to hurry if we're going to get there before him."

---

Finn tossed his jacket on the hook when they entered the condo ten minutes later, only stopping to grab the box of Charleston Chews from the inside pocket. Mila made a beeline for her room, tossing her jacket on the counter as she passed. Penny took off before she was thrown by Mila's fast movements.

"Can you hang my coat up, hon?" She shouted over her bare shoulder as she disappeared through her door.

Finn chuckled. "Sure. I didn't think you would be so nervous about seeing your old professor." He picked up her jacket and hung it beside his own.

"It's not that I'm nervous to see him. I like Gregory, it's just...he was my professor. At work, that's fine, but having a mentor in your house is a little nerve-wracking. I want to put on something less, I don't know, 'just gone out for drinks.'"

Finn went to the fridge and pulled out a beer, pulling the top off with his free hand before opening the box of Chews and tilting the box over his mouth and dropping a few in.

"Chi?" Penny asked, standing on the counter, one hand on her hip and the other open and reaching for the box.

Finn handed the yellow box over and took a drink of beer. He opened his mouth to make a comment, but then the intercom beside the door buzzed, and Finn walked over and hit the button to talk.

"Hello?"

"Hello? Finn?" An elderly voice crackled over the speaker.

"Gregory?"

"Open the door, my boy. I'm freezing my sagging balls off out here."

Finn's eyes went wide at the comment, and he started

chuckling as he hit the button, buzzing the elderly professor in. "Come on in. We're on the fourth floor."

There was no response, but the light that said the door was open went off, and Finn assumed he had entered the building.

After a minute or two, the doorbell rang, and Finn pulled it open, revealing the thin, distinguished figure of Gregory Hoffensteffer. He had a stack of books, binders, and loose papers in his arms, and gave Finn a broad toothy smile.

"Where's your coat?" Finn asked, seeing that the man only wore slacks and a black sweater that hung off of him as if it were a size too big.

Gregory walked by Finn and into the kitchen. He set the stack on the counter with a sigh of relief. "I forgot about it. I was in such a hurry to get here I left straight from my office, and didn't think about the fact that we would appear in the street outside."

"We?" Finn asked, opening the fridge and offering Gregory a beer.

"No, thank you. Yes, we. I have a friend who agreed to teleport me for the evening. Luckily she's a bit of a night owl, so getting home shouldn't be a problem. Unless you can teleport me?"

"Sorry, but dwarves can't teleport. We're too tied to the ground. Need a little air magic in there for teleporting." Finn mystically waggled his fingers. "Would you like some coffee or tea?"

"Tea would be great, my boy. Where's Mila?"

"I'm here," Mila called, coming out of her room, her dress replaced with a thick white sweater over the black leggings. Finn noted that she was now barefoot and probably was in the process of changing her pants when Gregory showed up and decided to go with it.

"Mila!" Gregory said in a sing-song voice, coming around the counter and wrapping her in a hug. "I'm so glad you came to me with this Valkyrie business. I always knew there was something special about you."

Mila hugged the old man, a smile on her face. "Thanks. I'm glad you came."

Finn put a kettle of water on the stove as he watched the reunion. "Are you hungry? I was going to make us some dinner."

Gregory nodded. "I would love some food if you don't mind. Oh, Penny! I didn't see you there. How have you been?" He held out a finger for her to shake.

She held the box of Chews to the side and gave his digit a pump or two with a taloned hand. "Shir shee. Chi chi."

"She says it's good to see you again," Mila translated.

"You've learned her language?" Gregory seemed impressed.

Mila shrugged. "She's been helping me, but it's mostly magic." She let out a laugh. "Like most things in my life recently."

She led him to the table, and they both sat as Finn opened the fridge and looked at what they had on hand.

"What sounds good, Penny?" Finn asked, keeping his voice down as to not interrupt the professor and his former pupil.

Penny hopped up onto his shoulder and scanned the fridge. Finally, pointing at the meat drawer. "Shir."

Finn pulled the drawer open and saw there was a bag of

raw shrimp. "When did we get these?" He asked Penny who did most of the shopping online and had it delivered. "You want me to grill 'em up or something?"

"Chi. Squee," Penny said as if he were an idiot.

"Scampi?" He considered, nodding as the idea grew on him. "Sounds good. I think I saw a baguette in the pantry. Why don't you slice that up while I get this started."

Penny licked her lips and nodded. She launched to the pantry door. Using her momentum, she grabbed and turned the knob, swinging the door open in a blur of movement.

"That's one way to do it," Finn commented, pulling a bag of jumbo shrimp out. He headed for the sink.

"Shir chi, chi?" Penny asked with a huff.

Finn thought about it. "I guess that really is your only option. Maybe we should install lever handles instead of knobs on all the doors. That way, you could just land on the handle to unlatch them."

Penny gave him a blank look then nodded enthusiastically. "Squee."

Finn chuckled. "Even I have brilliant ideas sometimes."

Penny gave him a shrug while making an indifferent face. "Eh."

He threw a raw shrimp at her.

Quick as a hawk, her cheeks puffed, and she blew a flame at the raw meat, cooking it thoroughly before catching it in her mouth.

"Cheeky little…" Finn laughed and continued to clean the prawns.

## CHAPTER SIX

Mila smiled, tucking one foot under herself, as she gained a little height in her seat to lean over the open book between her and Gregory. It had been a long time since she thought of herself as a student, but having her old mentor there, explaining new things to her in his rich teaching voice, brought her right back to those years in undergrad.

"Most of the myths surrounding Valkyries are an amalgamation of several cultures, but none of them is the full picture." Gregory indicated some notes he had written in the margin of a book on Norse artifacts. "For example, the Norse belief that is common today is clearly, at least partly, derived from the Shield Girls of Celtic folklore. One could say the entire concept of Valhalla is derived from the Celts, but that's another tangent altogether." He chuckled, the joke either too intricate or not funny enough. He cleared his throat and continued, "Anyway. The point being many legends of Valkyrie exist in ancient cultures—interestingly not so many in modern cultures. Now granted, the Norse culture of the period we consider the Viking age is not that old, all things considered, but the beliefs they held are from much further back."

Mila cleared her throat, trying to piece this all together. "Sorry, Professor, but how does this help me?"

Gregory leaned back and gave her a sour look. "How many times do I have to tell you to call me Gregory? You and I are colleagues. Would you like me to start calling you Dr. Winters?"

Mila laughed. "No. Please don't, *Gregory*. I'm sorry, it's a force of habit." She looked over the open books in front of them. "I don't want to sound ungrateful, but I already know most of this. I may have focused on Native American cultures in my postdoc, but my last assignment at the museum, my current assignment, I guess, is cataloging Viking relics. I did extensive study in preparation, and to be honest, I've read almost everything I can on Valkyries since I found out I am one." She gave him a sheepish look. "I need to know the story behind all this, not the legends."

Gregory nodded, a smile spreading across his face. "Apologies. I'm so used to teaching. I forget that not everyone needs the lesson." He pulled out a binder and leafed through a bundle of handwritten notes. "A few years ago, I started a deep study on several mythological creatures. All creatures are based on something real, even if the first thing isn't close to the final product. When I was introduced to the world of magic, I realized most of these myths were probably based on things much more similar to the end product. Ah, here we go." He opened the binder, removed a folder, and handed it to Mila, who began spreading out the contents on the table.

"This looks really old. When did you make these?" Mila asked, fingering the discolored papers.

Gregory thought about it for a second. "Probably around 1932. I know it was before the Second World War, but I can't remember when exactly. At the time, I was traveling through northern Europe, gathering notes on everything I came across. I found an old abandoned monastery out in the middle of nowhere. I'm not even sure what country I was in at that point. There was a pretty harsh winter storm brewing, so I decided to take shelter. To my surprise, there was a group of women already inside. They invited me in, and we chatted for quite a while. My ring was a big topic of conversation." He said, holding up the hand with a thin golden ring. "My extreme age let them know I was at least in the know when it came to magic. They never said what they were, but I always had a sneaking suspicion they were Valkyries. As they told me their story, the pieces fit. Mind you, I didn't put that together until much later."

Mila's eyes were wide. "You actually met some other Valkyries? What were they like?"

"Polite," Gregory said with a grin. "They provided me with a meal and pleasant conversation. They said they were traveling and needed to relocate their sisterhood. I got the impression that they were keeping some secrets or things safe. Without getting too into the details, I gleaned that they were not related in any way, except that they were all the same type of being. I asked if their families needed to keep themselves secret as well, but to a one, they claimed there was nobody else in their family like them. I took this to mean that their powers weren't hereditary, but passed on to them in some way."

Mila cocked her head, reading some of the notes while listening. "So, being a Valkyrie isn't something their mothers were? Interesting. Does that mean the power is like a parasite or symbiont? At least I know calling my mom and asking her would be a bad idea." She chuckled.

"I don't know how it works, but it was pretty clear that none of them did anything in particular to gain the powers," Gregory confirmed.

The smell of garlic and toasted bread began driving Mila mad with hunger. Just when she was about to get up and grab a cheese stick to hold her over, Finn came around the counter and put down a large bowl of pasta and another filled with shrimp covered in a buttery sauce that made Mila's mouth water.

"Take a break and have some food," Finn said, going back for plates as Penny flew over slowly with a plate covered in a sliced sourdough baguette for dipping in the butter sauce.

"This looks wonderful, Finn. Thank you." Gregory said, clearing the books and papers to the side as Finn put down plates for everyone.

"Not a problem. A fed body is a productive one. I figured it would help with studying," Finn said, filling the first plate with pasta and scampi and passing it to the old man.

Once everyone had a plate, they all dug in, silence the number one indicator of how good it was. Mila was deep in thought as she ate. If the powers of a Valkyrie were not hereditary, then how were new candidates chosen, and why had no other Valkyries ever approached her? Clearly, they could find one another if they were in a group when Gregory had met them. Maybe they didn't know about her? Or perhaps they didn't want to find her. That thought made her feel like she had done something wrong. Maybe they would find her now that she had awakened to her powers.

"Gregory, did you notice if any of them could talk to insects?" Mila asked, one of her eyebrows rising with curiosity.

Gregory cocked his head in contemplation. "Not insects, at least that I could see, but several of them seemed to have an affinity for different animals. Their leader had a large crow on her shoulder; she seemed to be able to communicate with. And I did catch several wolves out at the edge of the tree line, but when I mentioned it, the women were not concerned in the least. Each of them seemed to have some affinity to nature in some way."

Mila nodded. That was one mystery solved, at least. Sort of.

"Was there anything you could tell us about how they used their magic?" Finn asked, moping up the last of his butter sauce with a bread crust.

Gregory shook his head. "We didn't get into how their magic worked, and I only saw one spell from them during our short time together. The one thing I can say is that it was unlike any other magic I had come across. The power in it was of a pure white, and they didn't use any kind of bubble containment like most races do."

"That's not so unusual," Finn commented. "We dwarves

don't use bubble magic either. In fact, a lot of races forgo the bubbles. Even some elven magic is done on the fly."

"I never understood that," Mila said, reaching over and taking a sip of Finn's beer.

"Bubbles are one of the reasons Peabrains are so powerful," Finn said, pushing his clean plate away from him and leaning back. "They can form magic through the power of thought, where I have to use will directly on an object. The Bubbles make them more flexible in their casting and potentially more creative. Other races started using them exclusively, like the Huldu."

"So, you could use bubble magic if you wanted?" Mila was interested in this development.

Finn shook his head. "Not me, but Penny can. Dwarves are too connected to the earth and elements. For a time, we tried, but it was too much of a change, and we started losing our connection to the ground. Magic is a bit like pants."

Mila chuckled. "Pants?"

Gregory started taking notes.

Finn nodded, and Penny put a hand to her forehead, shaking her head in a defeated manner.

"You haven't even heard my theory, Penny." Finn grumped before continuing. "Yeah, like pants. Some pants are better suited for certain activities. Your leggings, for example, are very versatile. They stretch and keep you warm; you can use them when you dress up, or when we work out in the dojo. Jeans, on the other hand," he plucked at the dark blue material he was currently wearing, "they're tough and rugged. It takes a lot to tear them, but some activities are not great for them, like working out. Then there are slacks," he pointed to the charcoal-colored pants Gregory was wearing, "which are great for professional settings and carry an air of distinction to them, but they don't really provide warmth or durability. Different kinds of magic are like that. Some are better suited for flexibility, some for toughness and attack, and some for learning and expanding knowledge."

They all stared at him except for Gregory, who had his head down and was taking notes furiously.

"What, it's a good theory." Finn shrugged.

"That actually made sense," Mila stated, a little surprised.

## CHAPTER SEVEN

Finn awoke, yawning and smacking his lips. Mila was still breathing slow and steady, deep in sleep. Her head was on his right arm, pinning him to the bed. He reached over with his free hand and stroked the top of her head affectionately, eliciting a small groan as she curled up tighter, moving her head off his arm long enough that he could extract it. He smiled and leaned over to give her head a kiss.

Rolling over he saw that it was six thirteen in the morning. Far earlier than the dwarf liked getting up, although his early morning workouts with Danica, while she adjusted to her new arm, had trained his body that it was past time to be up.

With a deep breath, he swung his feet to the floor and stretched his back, getting the blood flowing. Pulling on a pair of thin workout pants and a black tee-shirt, he quietly padded out of Mila's room and closed the door behind him.

The sound of wet smacking made him glance over

towards Danica's room, and he was amused to see her and Phil kissing as he was clearly trying to leave. They noticed him and quickly separated, Danica, pulling her robe tighter around herself.

"Hey there, Finn. Didn't hear you get up." Danica said, her face turning red.

"Don't mind me, just going to make some coffee. You two want any?"

Phil chuckled. "I would love some, but I have to get to the hospital." He turned back to Danica. "See you tomorrow?"

She leaned over and kissed him quickly on the lips. "You bet. Have a good day."

Finn let them have their moment together, and went into the kitchen, fishing the bag of coffee beans from the freezer and scooping some into the grinder.

Phil passed by the kitchen, reaching for the door. "Uh, I'll see you later, Finn."

"Have fun at the morgue, Phil," Finn said, waving goodbye.

Phil chuckled. "I will."

Danica came over and sat on one of the stools at the island counter, her short robe now tied in place. "I'll take some of that." She said, looking over the various papers still spread out on the table. "What were you guys doing last night?"

"Oh, the papers?" Finn asked, pausing the conversation while the grinder did its loud work. "Mila's old professor stopped by and gave what info he has on Valkyries. I went to bed hours before he left, but I figured you two had gotten back before they were done."

Danica shook her head. "Nope. We haven't technically been to bed yet. After the bar, we took an Uber out to a friend of Phil's and played Mario Kart all night. We got home about an hour ago. Maybe an hour and a half."

"Lanky guys usually are built for endurance," Finn commented, not noticing Danica's face flushing crimson as he filled the coffee maker with the grounds and turned it on.

"So, what did you find out?" Danica asked, changing the subject.

Finn shook his head. "Not a ton. You should ask Mila when she gets up, she and the professor were up for hours talking after I was out."

The smell of coffee began to fill the condo, making Finn more alert just from the aroma. He opened up the freezer and pulled out one of the dozens of boxes of Charleston Chew minis. After opening the box, he dumped a small handful into his cup and shook the box at Danica.

"You want some in your coffee?"

She furrowed her brow. "You know what? Yes. I'll give it a try. Phil only drinks his coffee that way now. May as well see what all the fuss is about."

Finn grinned and dumped some in her cup as well. "That a girl. You never know what you don't like unless you try it."

"So, what's the plan for finding the Dark Star?" Danica asked, scratching at her bare ankle.

Finn frowned, leaning a hip on the counter and crossing his arms as he stared at the coffee maker, slowly dripping the black brew into the pot. "Not sure, but I think I'll give Preston a call. Hermin mentioned that he had given the info about the tracking spell to him, and if I know Preston, he didn't sit on the lead. Maybe he has something we can act on."

Danica snorted. "If someone would have told me, a few months ago, that my friends were going to be on a first-name basis with one of the richest men in the world, I would have bet the farm that they were wrong."

"Preston is just a guy with means. The fact that he does what he can to help others with that means is what I respect about him. Shit, we have money, it doesn't change who we are on the inside."

Danica raised an eyebrow. "You have money, I still have to go to work, eventually."

Finn raised an eyebrow at her. "You have it too. We're family now. Family takes care of one another. You did get the bank card from Penny, right?"

She blinked. "I thought that was for emergencies."

Finn laughed. "As far as I can tell, everything we do is an emergency. We literally have an armband that makes gold. What are we going to do, run out of money?"

She chuckled. "Well, that's true. I don't want to be a burden. I can work, so I should."

"True. Hard work is a reward all its own, but never think you're a burden. You lost an arm protecting Mila. I think you earned anything you want, in my eyes."

The pot was full enough, so Finn pulled it off the hot plate and filled both their cups. He stirred the candies in, then slid the mug over to Danica.

She was messing with her prosthetic, still wrapped in a concealment spell. She stopped when Finn set the mug in front of her. Danica took a sip and considered the chocolaty sweet coffee. "It's a bit like a vanilla mocha." She smiled and took another sip. "Well, done."

He held up his mug in cheers, and they both drank.

"I'm going to go take a shower," Danica announced, standing up. "I may be tired, but I may as well not look like a monster as well." She turned and headed for her room.

"Hey, Danica." Finn stopped her. "Why don't you take the card and go on an emergency shopping trip."

She raised an eyebrow. "What do you need?"

"Nothing in particular. I was thinking more for you. You've been cooped up in here for a week doing nothing but training. Think of it as a free test run for your new arm."

She smiled. "I think I can do that." She took a few steps, then turned. "Thanks, Finn. You're pretty good at this family stuff. If I had a big brother, I would want him to be like you."

Finn smiled. "You do have a big brother like me. It's me."

She chuckled. "I suppose you are." She held up the mug. "Thanks for the coffee."

"No problem."

---

Finn stepped out onto the balcony, breathing in the cold winter air. It had snowed a little overnight, and the city was coated in a fresh layer of white powder, muffling the sounds of the town and making him feel like he was the only living being in a hundred miles. With a free hand, he cleared the dusting of snow from under the awning and metal chair before taking a seat.

Sipping at his coffee, he squinted at the brilliant morning light bouncing off the snow-covered rocky mountains. He took a few minutes to enjoy the peace before pulling his phone out and scrolling through the contacts and finding Preston Meriwether's number. He hit the connect button, then put the phone on speaker, and set it down on the table, before taking another long drink of coffee.

After one ring, Preston picked up. "Finn. I was literally punching in your number to call you."

"Well, that's convenient," Finn said, putting his feet up on the rail. "What can I do for you?"

"I assume you're calling about this Dark Star business the Huldu brought to my attention?" Preston prompted.

"Yeah, they kept getting a hit on Boulder for some reason. Did you find anything?"

"We did." It sounded like Preston was using his keyboard in the background. "I just got a report from my people. We had a few images of Hellena from the battle you fought out on the ice. The cabin has several high-resolution cameras, and a few were good enough to get facial recognition software working on them. But the Boulder connection was the key. We ran every image we had connected with the city; old school photos, yearbooks, employment photos, you name it, and we got a hit."

"That's great," Finn said. "So, we know who she is?"

"Well, that's where things get interesting," Preston said, a frown evident in his tone. "We did find a match for a Hellena Hess, but it doesn't make any sense. There was a professor by that name at the University of Colorado Boulder, and her employee photo matches perfectly. And I mean perfectly. She looks exactly the same as in the photo."

"Well, that's good, right? At least you know for certain it's her."

"That's the problem. The photo was from twenty years ago. If this is the same person, then she's in her mid-fifties but looks like she's barely in her thirties. Granted, some people have good genes, but no one looks this similar after twenty years. Oh, and one more thing, according to every record we can find, she's dead."

Finn raised an eyebrow. "Dead?"

"Yeah. Died in a car crash twenty years ago. Drove off a cliff late one night, by the time they found her, it had been months, and there wasn't much left. The DNA samples matched her, though, so according to the state, she's dead." Preston took a sip of something and continued. "We did find a living relative still in Boulder, a Herman Hess, her brother. She also has a niece who's a senior at the university, Herman's daughter, Stephanie Hess. Other than that, we can't find anything. Parents are both dead, no cousins, just the brother."

"Do you think it's worth looking into? I seriously doubt her brother's going to know where she is," Finn said.

Preston was quiet for a few seconds. "I think it's worth looking into. Even if he hasn't seen her, there's at least some kind of connection. Besides, maybe they're a lot closer than we think. Hell, she might be on his couch right now, healing away."

Finn chuckled. "That would be nice and easy, so probably not what's going to happen. I'll head up there today and check it out."

"Okay. I have my guys on standby if the shit hits the fan. Try not to tear the city down while you're there? Boulder wouldn't be cheap to rebuild." Preston chuckled.

"No promises," Finn grunted, before hanging up.

Mila stepped out onto the balcony, her fluffy robe pulled tight against the cold, and a steaming cup of coffee in her hands. "Who was that?" she asked sleepily.

"Preston. We have a lead." He stood, putting his phone in his pocket and turning to her. "How do you feel about a trip up to Boulder?"

She chuckled. "For a second, I thought you were going to name some exotic place. Boulder's like twenty minutes away."

Finn frowned. "I thought it would be at least a half-hour or more."

"Not the way I drive." She grinned over the lip of her mug.

# CHAPTER EIGHT

Finn knocked on the little door to Penny's room that was halfway up the wall and sized for her. After a few minutes, and the sound of something crashing to the floor, the door opened, and Penny stood there, rubbing the sleep from her eyes.

"Chi?" she groggily mumbled.

"We have a lead in Boulder. Not sure how long we'll be up there, but you might want to pack a few things," Finn said.

Penny looked down at herself then back up at him. "Shir. Shee?"

Finn chuckled. "I know you don't wear clothes, I was thinking more of your gadgets. The comms you brought up to the lake were helpful. I was thinking something along those lines."

Penny's mouth made an O-shape, and she nodded before stumbling back and closing the door. A few seconds later, the large door to her room, beside the small one, opened, and she kicked a black duffel bag. "Chi chi." She let out a huge yawn that ended in a puff of flame.

"You want some coffee?" he asked, picking up the duffel. "There's a pot on the counter still steaming."

Penny brightened at that and took two hops before flapping her wings and flying for the kitchen. Finn followed her across the dojo towards the living room.

Danica came out of her room, dressed in leggings and a stylish gray sweater that hung off one shoulder. Her hair had been blown out straight and shined golden in the morning light.

Dropping the duffel full of tech gear on the couch, Finn smiled at Danica. "So, you decided to go shopping?"

She nodded. "Yeah, I could use a little retail therapy. Plus, I need to get a few more pairs of leggings."

"Aren't leggings like half your wardrobe?"

"You can never have enough leggings."

"I think Mila would agree with that."

"Agree with what?" Mila asked, coming out of her room, dressed for their trip in maroon leggings and a teeshirt.

"See? Barely see her in anything else." Finn said with a wave of his hand at her legs.

Mila gave him a narrow gaze. "Are you going on about leggings again? I think you're jealous that you can't get away with wearing them…in public, at least."

Danica laughed. "Oh, man. I would pay good money to see him in leggings at the bar."

Finn grumbled but didn't disagree. "Can you do me a favor, Danica?" He changed the subject.

"Sure. What do you need?" She said, wiping a tear of

laughter from her eye as she sat on the small bench where their shoes were stored in little cubbies along the front.

"Kevin is going to be stopping by tomorrow to go over the plans for the building remodel. We just got a lead on the Dark Star, and we're going up to Boulder to see what we can find. Can you meet with him and look the plans over and make changes if needed?"

She seemed surprised. "You want *me* to make changes? I figured that would be something you would want to approve."

"I trust your judgment. But, if you wouldn't mind, can you call Remmy and make sure she and her tribe leader are there too? They're getting a floor of their own, and I want to be sure it fits their needs. Let her know she can make any changes she wants, but that it has to be within reason. No golden toilets or anything crazy like that."

"How long will you be up in Boulder?" Danica asked, zipping up a pair of calf-high boots.

"Should only be a day, but you know how things can go. Could be a few days."

"Sure. I can handle looking over the plans. Hey, Mila. Do you need anything from the mall? I'm going shopping, and this big guy is footing the bill. So, it's my treat."

Mila considered, then plucked at her leggings. "I could use a few more pairs of leggings."

Finn rolled his eyes and laughed.

Penny raised an eye ridge. "Squee shir? Chi chi shee."

Mila put her hands on her hips and glared at Finn. "She's right. You love the way I look in leggings. Quit complaining."

"I do like the way you look in leggings." Finn waggled his eyebrows.

Mila made a slightly disgusted face. "Creep."

"I can't win." Finn shook his head. "I just can't win."

Mila came over and slapped him on the butt. "Oh, you won already. You got a very opinionated prize is all."

---

The trip to Boulder took about twenty minutes, confirming Mila's lead foot. She was convinced that it would have been under twenty, but Finn had made her stop for snacks.

"You know we don't always have to stop for food," Mila complained, eating a pretzel.

Finn and Penny both gave her a shocked look.

"You're the one who ate a whole bag of pretzels. Penny and I only shared a box of Chews. Besides, it's tradition."

"I did not eat a whole bag of pretzels." She slapped his leg.

Finn held up the bag and shook it. There were three pretzels left along with the salty powder. "You're right. It wasn't a *whole* bag."

She chuckled. "I can't help it. Ever since my magic has woken up, I can't get enough food. I'm always hungry."

"Yeah, that happens. Magic still needs power, and food is a pretty good source." He fished out the last three pretzels. "May as well finish 'em off. Don't want people to think you're a quitter."

Mila looked at the offered snacks, and Finn could see

she was trying to come up with a reason not to take them, but eventually, she huffed and took them.

Finn chuckled and looked at his phone. "The map says the house is around the corner."

Mila paused at the stop sign and checked the intersection before turning left down a dead-end street in the neighborhood they had been making their way through.

The houses were the small post-war ones that seemed to have been built by the hundreds overnight. They all had a large yard and detached garage beside identical floor plans. Finn read off house numbers. "202. 216. There it is, 224. Pull up out front."

"There's a car in the drive, he must be home," Mila said, pointing at the newer model SUV parked in front of the garage. "What's this guy's name?"

"Herman," Finn said, watching the house for movement.

Mila raised an eyebrow. "As in the author?"

Finn shrugged. "I don't know what he does. So how do we want to do this?"

Mila considered. "You could go around back with Penny while I check the basement windows."

Penny raised an eye ridge at them. "Chi? Shir squee."

"I guess we could do that."

"Yeah, knocking on the front door is a pretty good plan. I kinda forgot we don't know if he knows anything. Probably the civil approach is best."

Finn chuckled. "Ready?"

They climbed out of the car and made their way up the concrete path that cut through the front lawn to the front door. Mila was out front, and Finn and Penny brought up the rear. Penny rode his shoulder but hunkered down to look less threatening.

Mila took a deep breath and rang the bell.

After twenty seconds she rang it again, but they didn't hear any movement in the house. Finn stepped to the side and cupped his hands on the front window, pressing his face to them.

"The lights are off, and it doesn't look like anyone is here. Kinda spartan too. Just a couch, chair, and TV. No pictures on the walls or anything."

"Chi." Penny tapped him on the head, her eyes closed as she sucked in a deep lungful of air through her nose. Her eyes snapped open. "Shir, shee!"

"Dark magic?" Mila asked. "You can smell that?"

Penny nodded. "Chi, chi."

Finn sniffed the air and caught the edges of what Penny was smelling. "Yeah, I'm getting it too. She's either here, or it's been recent." He looked around the dead-end street and didn't see anyone. "Let's go around back and see if we can get in. This might be more of a lead than we bargained for."

Mila nodded and lead the way around to the driveway. A chain-link fence between the house and garage had a gate that was unlocked. Finn opened it, scanning the back-yard, seeing the trimmed yard and swingset somehow felt creepy in its ordinary-ness after smelling the tainted magic coming from the house. Like a monster in a pretty mask.

They passed a well-used gas grill and a neatly wound up hose dusted with a light coating of snow. Finn held Mila back from going up the steps first.

"Let me go ahead of you, just in case," Finn said, protectively.

Mila pulled down the collar of her tee-shirt, the sun glinting off her mithril chainmail. "I'm good."

Finn smiled. "Still." He positioned himself squarely in front of the backdoor.

"What do we do now?" Mila asked, reaching back and pulling Gram out, but not activating the sword.

"Now we knock. Really hard."

Finn lifted a booted foot and slammed it into the wooden door.

# CHAPTER NINE

The wooden door burst open, slamming into the wall hard enough the glass shattered and rained down on the '70s-ish linoleum.

"If he's home, he knows we're here," Mila said.

Penny nearly gagged when the rotten smell of dark magic bled out. Finn's nose wrinkled, and even Mila gave a small cough.

"Dark magic for sure," Finn commented, stepping inside, and pulling out Fragar, keeping the folded weapon at his side. "Herman?" he called, as he stopped in the dusty kitchen.

No answer.

"Looks like this place hasn't been used in months." Mila wiped a finger across the counter, a thick build-up of dust and grime sticking to it.

"You smell that?" Finn asked.

"You mean something beyond the smell of rot? No, I can't really smell anything besides that." Mila sniffed, just to be sure and almost sneezed.

"Chir shee," Penny said, inhaling the air.

"Yeah. Death," Finn agreed.

"How the hell can you pick that out over the general smell of nastiness?" Mila said, shaking her head.

"Your senses will sharpen with time. Give it a few months." He sniffed a few more times, but Penny was the one who pointed to a door off the kitchen. "Agreed. Basement."

They moved to the door, and Finn pulled it open. The smell of rotten meat hit them like a wall.

Mila gagged. "Ugh." She put her arm up over her nose.

"You going to be okay?" Finn asked her.

She nodded and shooed him down the steps.

"I'm surprised there are no flies," Mila observed.

"They must have been driven off by the dark magic," Finn said, peering into the darkness.

"Probably. Flies are smarter than people give them credit for. Do you know how far away meat has to be for them not to smell it?"

Finn shook his head. "How far?"

"I'm not sure, but it's a long way. If they aren't here, then something's up."

Reaching over, Finn flipped the light switch, but nothing happened. He flipped it up and down a few times before giving up on the idea. The dwarf descended the narrow wooden steps one at a time. He sensed Mila behind him, then felt her hand touch his back to keep balance.

What he could see from the light filtering down from the kitchen showed a bare stone floor and unpainted cinder block walls. He figured the basement was never used for more than storage and, if the musty smell that accompanied the rot was any indication, maybe a washing machine.

There was a muffled, repeating squishing sound barely audible, making Finn heft Fragar a few inches higher.

Reaching the bottom of the steps, Finn's eyes began to adjust, his dark vision finally kicking in. While he could see better than Mila, who he guessed couldn't make anything out, the darkness was thick enough, he was having trouble picking out details.

"Screw this," Finn mumbled before kneeling and putting his palm to the stone floor. He focused his magic and breathed a word. "*Aotrom.*"

The entire floor glowed softly with white light. Over a few seconds, the room went from pitch black to bright as a cloudless noonday.

Mila and Finn gasped as they saw the source of the rotting smell. Dozens of half-eaten rats littered the floor. Small pools of blood surrounded the discarded half bodies, looking particularly ominous as the only light was coming from below.

"I guess we know where the smell is coming from," Finn said, standing.

Mila squatted in front of a rat. "Something bit this in half. See here? Those are from human teeth."

Finn frowned and scanned the room. There were no other parts to the basement, just the one place. An old washer and dryer sat to one side, with a large slop sink next to them. It looked like a pile of dirty clothes was stacked waist-high between the appliances and sink. An extended workbench was built into the opposite wall. Next to it, an overturned stool and some spilled paint cans. A metal cabinet on the back wall had a bent door where it looked like someone had taken a sledgehammer to it.

"Doesn't look like much down here," Mila said, standing and backing from the half-eaten rat. "Someone came down here and ate a few dozen rats then left? What the fuck is going on?"

Finn shook his head. "I have no clue. Let's check the rest of the house."

Penny sniffed the air again. "Chi." She held up a hand, indicating they should wait. After a second, she spread her wings and pushed off Finn's shoulder. Slower than should be possible for a creature her size, that was beating its wings as quiet as she was, she hovered around the room, sniffing out whatever it was that her extra sensitive nose smelled.

"What is it?" Finn asked.

Penny held up a hand, forestalling the question as she approached the washing machine. She sniffed and lowered herself towards the pile of clothes, her eyes narrowing.

The basement was silent, even Penny's magical wings weren't making a sound. Finn cocked his head, listening for the squishing sound that he had heard on the way down the steps, but he couldn't hear it anymore. He looked at the dead rats, and his eyes went wide. The sound had been something biting into raw meat.

"Penny, get back!" Finn shouted, stepping forward, and whispering Fragar's power word. The ax folded open in a flash of blue and purple magic just as the pile of clothes twisted and stood.

Penny shot backward as a dark brown, melted hand snatched for her, missing by a few inches. The thing wasn't a pile of clothes at all, but a half-melted human shape with the remnants of clothes hanging off of it. Deep red eyes were set in what looked like melting clay. It opened its mouth far more than a human could, and a keening sound pierced the air, making Finn flinch as the sound threatened to rupture his eardrums.

Turning, the abomination locked eyes with Finn. An evil grin showed a row of blood-covered human teeth, and a half-eaten rat fell from its bloody hand to plop on the floor.

Faster than Finn thought possible, it leaped across the room and slammed into him. On pure instinct, Finn raised the flat of Fragar between them, using the full blade as a shield from the thing's mouth. Mila was shoved to the side as Finn and the creature slammed into the wall.

The clacking of teeth let Finn know if he hadn't gotten Fragar up, the thing would be chomping into his neck.

Bony fingers dug into Finn's shoulder and arm, making him grunt in pain. He shoved as hard as he could, but the creature wouldn't budge.

"Shit, this thing is strong," Finn grunted, shoving for all he was worth.

Suddenly the abomination's right arm went limp, and he was able to shove it off. In the split second that it flew through the air, Finn saw Mila had used Gram to slice its arm clean off. The detached arm fell to the ground and melted into a pool of black and brown muck that hissed on the stone floor.

To their horror, the creature got to its feet, its right arm already growing back, but this time it was more bulbous and deformed, the hand ending in short talons instead of fingers.

Penny swooped in from behind, blasting it with dragon fire that engulfed its head and shoulders. When the flame died out, the creature, while burned black, seemed to be in no worse shape than before.

Finn roared and charged.

# CHAPTER TEN

Mila stepped back to give Finn room to fight, but she was against the steps and had little opportunity to help.

Finn was grappling with the horror, having gotten his ax stuck in the thing's midsection, where the brown putrid flesh healed over the blade, essentially swallowing the weapon. Now only the handle protruded at an odd angle from the thing's torso.

As far as Mila could tell, the fight was not going in Finn's favor. Usually, he was the strongest guy in a row, but Finn was struggling to match the creature. His face was red, and a blood vein pulsed on his forehead as he descended into the rage.

Finn spun and lifted the creature off its feet. He slammed it into the wall beside the stairs. Mila took the opportunity to stab the thing in the neck, but she couldn't tell if it did any good, besides eliciting a gurgling hiss that shot black blood from its mouth and onto Finn's face.

"Not helping," Finn grunted, shaking his head to get the black fluid out of his eyes.

"Sorry!" Mila shouted when she saw the goop running down his face and into his beard.

Penny landed on Mila's shoulder and blew another thin line of fire into the creature's face. It was either not affected by magic or fire, in particular, was ineffective. Penny hissed in annoyance and launched herself at the abomination's face. She raked her talons deep into the flesh. It roared and hissed, but otherwise, it never lost its focus on overpowering Finn.

"Going to need a hand here. It keeps getting stronger for some reason." Finn was down on one knee, his teeth grinding.

"Should I shoot it?" Mila shouted, jumping off the steps and putting a little distance between them.

"Whatever. That sounds good. Shoot it in the face." There was a distinct snapping sound, and Mila could see one of Finn's fingers bent at an odd angle, as their inter-locked hands twisted back and forth for an advantage.

Finn growled, his face turning redder, and his eyes narrowing. He let out an animal roar, forcing the creature up the wall as Finn stood to his feet. Now that his rage was in full swing, he became stronger, yet he still couldn't tear the thing apart, like he wanted to. Instead, it looked to Mila like a slow-motion dance as Finn overpowered the crea-ture, but was still forced to move its arms slowly. Mila couldn't imagine the forces being used.

She folded Gram back into its handle and snapped it into her holster, before pulling the Ivar pistol out. She checked the safety and aimed the runic, black steel pistol.

With Finn on his feet again, she couldn't get a shot without hitting him. The weapon's blast radius when her celestial power washed through it was unpredictable, making precision impossible.

"I don't have a shot, Finn. You're in the way." Mila tried to find an angle, but Finn was now in the thing's face, growling more than the creature, and Penny was doing her best to turn the thing's head into flesh ribbons by flying around it and digging long furrows in the molten, clay-like flesh.

Seeing it was not going to win this war of attrition between its two foes, the creature screamed and pulled its hand back hard enough, it ripped off at the wrist. The move unbalanced Finn. He stumbled to the side, slamming into the dryer, denting it with his hip. The detached hand melted in Finn's grip, while the creature's stump grew a deformed, twisted replacement; this one with four-inch talons.

It jumped, wrapping its legs around Finn's midsection and began ripping bloody chunks from his shoulder with the new talons.

Mila's heart jumped when Finn screamed in pain and rage. Blood arced from him and splattered across the floor and walls each time the creature's hand came down.

Penny slashed at the creature with talon and tooth but to no avail. She huffed flame and smoke, as her attacks picked up speed.

Mila dropped the Ivar. She held her hands in front of her like she'd seen casters do. She had no idea how to use her magic, but if she didn't do something, Finn was going to die. Not knowing what to do, she tried to will an answer into her hands, whatever that might be, but nothing happened.

Glancing up, she saw Finn had gone to one knee, his face pale and sweating.

Mila redoubled her efforts. She had to make this work. If Finn died, that thing would be free to tear her apart, too, eating her like it had the rats. The magic was there, she had used it before, she just needed to use it again.

Once again, she tried to will something into happening. It felt too broad of a request for her to focus on. Mila needed to be more specific. She visualized the drooping face screaming at Finn. Imagined it burned to ash. She wanted the power to banish the horror, to make it stop ripping chunks out of her love. She wanted it destroyed utterly.

She drew upon the power to destroy the creature. Mila gasped as her hands glowed soft white. She felt the flow of energy. It shot outwards from the back of her head, through her core, and out through her hands. She had no idea what the power would do, but she was excited that it was doing something. The intensity began to make her hands tingle after a few seconds, and she set her jaw, glaring at the creature as it stopped attacking Finn to stare at her glowing hands.

"You want some of this, bitch?" Mila sneered.

In a surprise move, it backed away from Finn, and Mila stepped up behind the groaning dwarf. Finn still had a grip on the creature's arm, and he was not letting go.

"Where you going? We haven't finished our dance." Finn slurred, pulling the arm in his hand back towards him.

The red beady eyes exhibited signs of panic, glancing around the room, looking for a way out. Finn's vice-like grip on its arm was too mighty. It raised its taloned hand to strike at the dwarf's fist.

Mila came forward, pressed up against Finn's ruined back, her teeshirt and leggings soaking in his blood. She reached over his kneeling form and grasped the abomination's head between her glowing hands.

"Fuck you," she growled, before pushing her power through its skull with everything she had.

The creature screamed, its jaw sagging before falling off as the whole body crumbled to black ash in the blink of an eye.

Finn fell backward, no longer able to hold himself up. Mila did her best to catch him, but he weighed too much and knocked her on her bottom, his head falling into her lap.

Penny landed on her back and pulled a healing potion out. Mila opened Finn's mouth while Penny scurried around to Mila's front and pried the stopper loose. Mila took the vial from Penny and poured it down Finn's throat.

"There you go." She soothed, watching him swallow the red fluid down.

"That was close," Finn croaked as the healing potion repaired his back.

"What the hell was that thing?"

He cleared his throat and began to move his arm, flexing the shoulder that was, a few seconds ago, no more than ground beef. With a little help, he sat up, pulling his bomber jacket off and looking it over with a frown.

"A homunculus." He peered at the pile of black ash.

"What's a homunculus?" Mila pulled scraps of Finn's black tee-shirt apart to get a look at his mending flesh. She wanted to make sure one healing potion was enough.

"Like a flesh golem, or a man created from spare parts. Usually, they need a constant feed of magic to remain alive, either from their creator or a device of some kind." Finn frowned. "It's not a spell used in polite society. It tends to be cruel for the homunculus, who is, by all metrics, alive and a real person. Something alive like that should not be held to the whims of a master."

Satisfied he was healing well, Mila focused on the conversation. "Then what happened to this one? Who would make a man that was so…grotesque?"

"I think this was Herman, but the spell keeping him alive got twisted somehow."

"Shir shee, squee," Penny suggested.

"I suppose it could have something to do with the way magic is acting up," Finn said, thinking through the process. "Maybe the spell that maintained the poor thing somehow got twisted. Then, in turn, it twisted the form. Either this was intentional and happened because Hellena was trying to kill us, or it was an accident, and we happened to be the ones that came across it. Either way, she needs to pay for what she did to this poor person."

## CHAPTER ELEVEN

Penny surprised both Finn and Mila by casting a spell that not only cleaned the clothes they were wearing but also mended them. Finn's ruined shirt crawled over him like an octopus caught on land, the tentacles of shredded cotton reaching across the holes to join together and thicken until there was no hole left. Blood and gore that coated Mila's clothes and Finn's face and beard evaporated, leaving only the pleasant smell of fresh-cut grass.

"Why the hell have you been hiding that spell all this time?" Finn asked, overjoyed that he wouldn't have to smell the bloody puke that had seeped into his beard during the fight. "Do you know how much we could have saved on new tee-shirts?"

Penny smiled, her teeth gleaming. "Suqee. Shir shee chi."

"Gwen? How did you get her to teach you something for free? I know I never gave you enough cash to convince her to teach you a spell. And I'm pretty sure she doesn't take credit cards."

"Shir. Chi, chi."

"Why would she bet against you being able to eat five tooters at once? That's like saying garbage disposals are only good for coffee grounds." Finn laughed. "Well, I must say, it's a damn good spell, and if you got five free tooters out of the deal, then it was even better."

Mila appeared a bit green at the mention of the sweet blue larvae. "Can we change the subject? I just got clean, I really don't want to puke."

"I can't believe you don't like tooters, just because they're larvae," Finn said in disbelief.

"Seriously, you need to stop." Mila's cheeks puffed behind a curled fist as she dry heaved.

Finn laughed and climbed to his feet, pulling his mended bomber jacket back on. "We should check the rest of the house. Maybe there's a clue that can lead us to Hellena."

Mila took his offered hand and pulled up, brushing dirt and dust from the seat of her leggings. "Good idea. Do you think there are more of those things around? I don't know if I could do that spell again."

Finn sniffed the air deeply, closing his eyes. "I don't think so. The corruption is dissipating now that it's gone. Plus, the power it takes to create a homunculus is ridiculous. I seriously doubt she made more than one."

Penny landed on Mila's shoulder as they started up the steps. Mila took one last look around, raising her eyebrow.

"What is it?" Finn asked, standing a couple steps below her and watching her think something over.

She pointed to the relatively empty basement. "This just looks, I don't know, too empty? My dad is pretty much a neat freak, and his basement has more in it than this one."

"Two things. First, it's good to know that your tidiness is hereditary and not some sort of pathology. Second, I don't understand what it is you're pointing out."

Mila rolled her eyes. "First," she mocked, "if I wasn't a neat freak, between you and Danica, we would be drowning in piles of dirty clothes and discarded mail. And, second, from what Preston told us, this brother of hers has been around for a long time, even has a daughter. Someone that has a kid and owns a house doesn't keep it this clutter-free, no matter how neat and clean they are. Besides, the dusty kitchen was enough to convince me a real person didn't live here."

Finn blinked. "I forgot about the daughter. It can't be his, he was a creature. Homunculi can't have kids."

Realization dawned on all three of their faces.

Mila put it into words. "The daughter isn't his. It's Hellena's!"

"Looks like we're heading to the university. Let's check the rest of the house. At this point, we can use every clue we can find."

They headed up the steps and spread out in the house, Mila taking the upstairs and Finn checking the rest of the first floor. Penny stayed in the basement to do a few spells on the homunculus's remains, looking for any kind of residual spell thread that could lead them to Hellena.

Finn walked up creaking, loose steps to find a short hall with one bathroom at the end of the building and three small bedrooms. Finn put his head into the first room—it was empty, as was the second, but the third was lined with transparent plastic sheets like some kind of serial killer den.

Finn raised an eyebrow, taking in the stainless steel autopsy table and trays of surgical tools so foreign to anything he had ever seen before he couldn't even guess at their purpose.

He stepped in and saw a large freezer chest against the wall and a desk with several dry-erase boards and cork-boards on the wall above it. Finn hesitated, unsure he really wanted to see what was in the freezer. Overcome with curiosity, he opened it slowly. Finn was half relieved and half horrified to see that there were no human body parts in it, but there were bodies. All manner of animal carcasses filled the chest, from a whole suckling pig to what looked like the haunch of a horse. He even saw a ziplock bag full of half dissected squirrels.

"Find anything...oh god. Is that a bag of squirrels?" Mila stopped, having just stepped into the room and her eyes locking on the bag in Finn's hand. Penny gave the bag a hungry look but locked onto the desk in the corner.

Hopping off Mila's shoulder, Penny flew to the desk, while Finn dropped the bag back into the chest of horrors.

"Yeah. I think this is where Hellena kept the raw mate-rials to maintain the homunculus. I've heard they tend to fall apart without regular maintenance." Finn scanned the raw materials, looking for anything that might help, but knowing there wasn't much a chest full of frozen meat could say. "She probably needed to update his appearance from time to time as he was aging."

"We need to be careful with the daughter. What was her

name?" Mila asked, taking in the impromptu surgical suite for the first time.

"Stephanie Hess. According to Preston's people, she just turned twenty-one a few weeks ago. But they didn't have much else on her. I think they were more focused on the brother."

"Well, the question is, does Stephanie know that her uncle is, or at least, was a monster? She could be innocent in all this, or an accomplice. We need to be careful about how we approach her."

"Chi!" Penny called out, waving them over to the desk.

Finn and Mila came over, and Penny pointed out the various photos on the corkboard. Finn leaned in, then opened up his phone and compared the photo Preston had sent of Herman to the ones on the board.

"This was definitely him. I have to say I'm impressed Hellena got away with this for so long. These pictures seem to cover the entire twenty years since her quote-unquote death."

Mila leaned toward one of the photos, then pulled it off the board. "This must be Stephanie. It looks like it's from a few years ago, but I can see a bit of resemblance between her and her mother. Have to say, the red hair is a surprise; must have come from her father's side."

Finn looked over Mila and saw a picture best described as uncomfortable. Herman was smiling woodenly and had his hand on what looked like a twelve-year-old Stephanie's shoulder as they stood in front of a row of rose bushes. The girl was rigid as if she didn't like to be touched, and she only had the barest of forced smiles, her shoulders half-cocked in a shrug.

"Is it just me, or is that photo staged as hell?" Finn asked. "He looks like a creepy stalker with that mustache."

"Shir chi." Penny snickered, landing on his shoulder.

Finn's eyes widened in shock. "I do not look like that in photos! I look great."

Mila sucked air in through her teeth, a pained expression on her face. "Actually, you don't. Sorry, babe, but you look like a wooden cutout in most photos."

Penny laughed, making Finn frown. "Really? I thought I was doing pretty good. For a dwarf, I'm very photogenic."

"Are there a lot of photos of dwarves to compare yours to?"

"Most dwarves are into having paintings done rather than photos."

"Maybe they know something you don't." She patted him on the arm. "Come on, we should get out of here. We need to find Stephanie and see if she knows anything."

Finn did a once-over of the desk. He picked out some notes regarding changes Hellena made to Herman over the years. It seemed nothing had been done in the last year, though.

"Okay, I don't know about you, but I could use a little food before we head onto campus," Finn said, leading the way out into the hall.

Penny brightened at that. "Chi, chi."

Finn gave her a sidelong glance. "Well, imagine that. Penny wants some food. Let me guess, the bag of squirrels got your tummy rumbling?"

Penny rolled her eyes, and Mila chuckled.

# CHAPTER TWELVE

Half an hour later, they sat down at a little diner just off campus, with a view of the university and mountains beyond. The red *pleather* upholstered booth had years of hastily repaired cuts and squeaked like they were full of mice when Finn and Mila slid into them.

After explaining Penny was a service animal and putting the little vest on her, the waitress took their orders, giving the dragon the side-eye the whole time.

Penny didn't help the process by giving the same look to the waitress.

Mila ordered a spinach and feta omelet while Finn got the "Gut Buster" special, which came on four plates. He didn't really want all the food, but he knew Penny would be picking over his when she finished her steak and eggs, so he over-ordered. It was the only way he got a full meal when they went out.

They ate in silence, each of them thinking about how best to approach Stephanie. The first problem was that they didn't know where she was exactly. Sure, she was on campus, but there were another thirty thousand people there along with her, and they didn't even know what school she was attending. The second problem was that they didn't really know what she looked like. They had the photo from the homunculus' house, but that was at least five years old.

Penny was polishing off Finn's biscuits and gravy, while Finn finished his meal with some sourdough toast slathered with strawberry jam over the melted butter when Mila let out a sigh.

"I have no idea how we find her. There are just too many people on campus. I guess we could just go sit out on the quad and look for all the redheads, but I feel like that's not very efficient," she said, her shoulders slumping.

"Wouldn't that look suspicious? Two adults sitting on campus intensely looking at all the redheads?"

"Yeah, I might be able to get away with it, but they would have words with you."

Finn's jaw dropped in mock outrage. "That's sexist!"

"I don't know if an honest threat assessment would be considered sexist. Pretty sure it doesn't work that way."

"Shir shee," Penny said, swallowing the last bit of biscuit before continuing, "Chi, squee shee."

"You *do* know to impersonate a federal agent is a severe crime, right?" Mila said, going pale at Penny's suggestion.

Finn, however, nodded. "I have my runic papers that would pass as an FBI badge. All we need is a printout of Stephanie's schedule. We would be in and out, easy."

Mila's eyes were a little wide. "This is a horrible idea."

"You have a better one?"

Mila thought it through, but before she could answer,

Finn's phone rang. He dug it out of his pocket and looked at the caller ID.

"Who is it?" Mila asked, finishing off her coffee.

"Preston," he said, before answering. "Hello."

"Finn." Preston sounded tired. "How are things going with the Dark Star hunt? Find anything at the brother's house?"

"Funny you should mention that. Turns out that the brother isn't real."

There was a beat of silence before Preston answered. "I have pictures of him. I'm pretty sure he's real. Did you go to the right house?"

"Oh, it was the right house, and there was something there. Turns out, the brother was a long con. He was a homunculus. Been around for at least twenty years, but in the last few weeks, became twisted and reduced to a monster stuck in the basement eating rats."

Preston was silent so long, Finn pulled the phone from his ear to be sure the call was still connected. "Preston? You still there?"

"Yeah," he said tiredly. "I'm here. Please tell me you took care of it? We can't have an uncontrolled homunculus running around Boulder."

"Mila took care of it, but you might want to send someone to clean up the house," Finn said, giving the waitress a nod and sliding his mug towards her when she approached with a coffee pot.

"Mila? How did she do that?"

"Used her Valkyrie magic. Honestly, we don't know exactly what she did, but it was pretty damn powerful.

Turned the thing to ash at a touch." Finn's voice held a hint of pride.

"She burned the thing to ash? At a touch?"

"Nope. Skipped the whole burning part, and went straight to the ashy leftovers. She was like that big purple guy when he snapped his fingers." Finn said, giving Mila a wink.

She just rolled her eyes.

"The big purple guy?"

"Squee shir," Penny said, helpfully.

"Thanos. Thanks, Penny. I was going to say Wrinkly Chins, but I knew that wasn't right."

"Wrinkly..." Preston sighed. "Okay, I'll send some people over to clean the place out. Wait, if he was a homunculus, does that mean his daughter is one too?"

Finn's eyes widened. "Honestly, I hadn't considered that, but I don't think so. We're working on the idea she is Hellena's daughter, and Herman was a cover story."

"I suppose that makes more sense." Preston thought for a second before saying, "I'll get my people on finding out what they can about her. Give me a day or two, and I'll send it over."

"I think we have a plan to meet her. We're going to stop by the university in a few minutes."

"You're on top of it. Good. I'll still get a couple people on it, too. Keep me informed. Now on to the thing I was calling about in the first place." Preston went from contemplative to all business in the matter of a sentence. "I have gotten several reports over the last few days of magic not responding like it should. Some people are reporting magic is completely random when casting, while others are saying they don't have access to their magic at all. I fear this is some kind of attack from our mutual friend, but for the life of me, I can't see how it would help her cause. Have you seen anything like this over the last few days?"

"I have a friend who brought it to my attention, but he said it was only a slight interruption or resistance. Penny has noticed it, too, but not to the point it's messing with her powers." Finn furrowed his brow. "We thought there would be more time before the magical public noticed anything."

"Why didn't you come to me earlier with this?" Preston pressed.

Finn shrugged, even though the Minotaur couldn't see it. "It wasn't serious enough to bother you with."

"Don't give me that shit. I know full well, you are not impressed with my wealth and position. Frankly, it's one of the reasons I trust you so much."

Finn chuckled. "That's true. Where I'm from, you're middle class. I didn't say anything to you because, frankly, I've been so used to doing things on my own I forget some people want to help. It wasn't an indictment on you. I just didn't think about it."

Preston snorted, the sound especially pronounced due to his bull nostrils. "I can understand that, but things are different now. This ship is your home; we are stronger if we work together."

Finn glanced over at Mila and Penny having a quiet conversation while he was on the phone. Mila was laughing while Penny juggled three creamers. Finn smiled. "You're right, Preston. We are stronger together."

"Damn right. So, if this is some kind of attack, what

would it accomplish? I thought Hellena's goal was to show that magicals need their own place in the world. Why mess with the very thing that sets them apart?"

Finn took a sip of coffee while he considered. "We have a theory that she might be trying to awaken a large number of people all at once. Cause a little havoc that the Huldu can't contain. If the world finds out about magicals, then there would be no turning back. I have no idea if it would work, but it aligns with her goals."

Preston was silent for a while. "That would be beyond bad. We're talking world-ending bad. We need to pinpoint where the anomaly is, and take it out. It has to be a device or spell that's causing it, and it obviously has a range limit. We're getting reports around the Denver area, but they are as far away as a hundred miles. The more reports we get, we will be able to narrow down where the heaviest concentration of disturbances are happening. Hopefully, that will point us in a direction to search."

"Okay, we'll go talk with Stephanie and shake something loose from this end," Finn said, pulling out his wallet and putting a couple twenties on the check the wide-eyed waitress had just left. She had caught Penny juggling, and her world had just gone insane.

"Out of curiosity, how are you going to find her?"

"Pretend to be an FBI agent and have the school print out her schedule," Finn said, matter of fact.

There was silence on the line, then a heavy sigh. "That is an incredibly illegal thing to do. I'll be sure if the university calls to check your credentials, they will check out. See, Finn, this is why we need to work together."

Finn chuckled. "That's helpful. Thanks, Preston. I'll let you know what we find."

"Sounds good. Tell Mila to be safe. She might have destroyed the homunculus, but she's still new to her powers. She needs to ease her way into them."

"Will do. Thanks again." Finn hung up, raising an inquisitive eyebrow at Penny, who was still juggling. "You clowns ready to go? Preston is covering for our FBI plan."

Penny tossed one of the creamers higher than the others, and hit it with her tail, sending it flying at Finn's face. He snatched it out of the air, crushing it, leaving creamer dripping between his fingers. Penny's eyes went wide in surprise as the other two creamers hit the table.

Mila burst out laughing, handing him a napkin. "Why on earth did you crush it?"

"Reflex."

Penny began laughing, not believing it had worked out so well.

# CHAPTER THIRTEEN

Once they were in the car, Mila spent a good ten minutes on her phone while they sat in the diner's parking lot.

Finn raised an eyebrow. "Are you playing that game again, or looking for something?"

She smacked his arm without looking away from the phone. "I'm not playing that game, though you did remind me I have to do the daily challenge. No, I'm looking for the fucking admin building. We can't just walk into any building and ask." She leaned over, showing Finn a map of the campus. "I think we can go here, but it kinda looks like a house. I'm trying to make sure this will work. Be patient."

"I am patience personified," Finn said, leaning back in his seat and pulling a box of Charleston Chews from his jacket pocket.

"Okay, I think this is the place. We have to drive around campus to get there, but at least they have a parking lot we don't have to pay for." She dropped her phone in the cupholder. She pulled the Hellcat out of the lot and gunned it. Traffic caught up to them, and someone honked.

"Crazy drivers," Mila complained, looking in the rearview mirror.

Finn and Penny shared a look. Finn was dumb enough to say something. "Didn't *you* pull out in front of *them*?"

Penny smacked her forehead.

Mila gave him a look so dirty he felt like he needed a shower. "I had room," she said, slowly and deliberately.

Finn, nonplussed, looked behind them at the car riding their ass, then over at Mila. "Clearly."

"I don't see you driving, bub."

"I'd like to give it a shot if you don't mind me driving your car. I mean, I have driven it, but I would like a little more practice."

This argument was not going Mila's way, and she knew it. "Maybe you should get something a little less powerful to practice with. Like a corvette."

"Maybe I should get a motorcycle," Finn said, staring off into the distance. "Those look fun as shit."

"Are you serious? They're death machines." Mila swerved into the next lane and passed a slow-moving pickup truck.

"Sweet. Death Machine…that's what I can name it."

She rolled her eyes. "Knowing you, you'll enchant it to drive on walls and run on starlight and dreams."

Finn cocked his head. "Not a bad idea."

"You know how to do that?"

"No, but it would be cool if I did." He winked at her before he and Penny burst into laughter.

"You guys suck." She patted the Hellcat's dash. "It's okay,

baby. We'll find some way to make you more fuel-efficient."

———

Finn stepped into the small lobby of the administration building and whipped his sunglasses off, imitating every crime procedural show he had ever seen. He cocked a hip and looked around the small room with narrowed eyes, spotting the receptionist who was staring at him with a perfectly groomed, raised eyebrow.

Mila squeezed between him and the door frame to get in the building and, tossing him a dirty look, walked up to the counter around the desk, leaning on it and giving the young woman there a smile.

"Sorry about my partner. He's new," Mila said, hiking a thumb at Finn.

"New to what?" she whispered, not taking her round eyes off of him.

Mila whipped out a piece of paper covered in runes and folded into fourths. Opening it like a badge, she showed the slightly glowing runes to the woman.

"New to the bureau." Mila gave her a wink.

"You're with the FBI? That's so cool." She said, her eyes going wide at the enchanted paper.

Finn, noticing that the conversation was moving along without him, snapped out of his pose, stepping forward. He held out his own folded paper, letting the receptionist get a good look at it before snapping it closed and tucked it into his back pocket.

"Miss, we're going to need a student's file. Schedule at

the least. Who do we need to talk to to get that done?" he said, in a pretty passable Big Jim McLain impression.

The young woman cleared her throat and smiled. "I can get that for you. Who's schedule do you need?"

Finn glanced at Mila and raised his eyebrows in surprise at how easy that was. Mila made a 'go on' motion with her hand.

"Oh, uh, Stephanie Hess," Finn said, giving the receptionist a smile and leaning an elbow on the counter surrounding the desk. "What's your name, by the way?"

The young woman began typing and flashed a smile. "Gretchen. I'm sorry, I didn't catch your names."

"Oh, I'm agent McLain, and this is agent," Finn glanced at Mila, his beard parting in a huge smile, "Vallon. We just wrapped up a big case in Hawaii chasing down some communists."

Mila raised an eyebrow, obviously confused. Finn realized she must not have seen the movie he was referencing. Granted, it wasn't one of the most famous Duke films, but it was worth seeing. He would have to sit her down and make her watch it with him.

"Communists?" Gretchen asked, spinning around and loading the printer's paper tray. "I thought the Red Scare was, like, a hundred years ago."

Mila rolled her eyes at Finn. "It wasn't quite a hundred years ago, but it was a long time ago. Far before our time." She gave Finn a knowing stare, trying to force him to stay on track. "Agent McLain is pulling your leg. We can't talk about our cases with civilians."

Pulling a couple of sheets from the printer, Gretchen turned and handed them to Mila. "Oh, that's funny," she said without humor. "I'll let the dean know you stopped by. We want to be helpful to law enforcement, but we still need to document everything. Is there a number where he can reach you if he has questions?"

Mila was prepared for the question and pulled out a small piece of paper with the number for the FBI headquarters in Washington. When Preston said he would take care of it, she had been much more into the idea.

Gretchen stared at the paper and nodded. "Okay. Let us know if there is anything else you two need."

Finn nodded, putting his sunglasses back on with a flourish. "The only thing we need is a case to follow and a bad guy to apprehend."

Gretchen cocked her head to the side and blinked in confusion.

Mila rolled her eyes. "Come on, McLain. We have bad guys to get. Thanks for all your help, Gretchen."

"Sure. No problem." She waved. "Have fun."

Mila led the way outside and turned on Finn as soon as they were out of view. "What the fuck was that all about? If that girl had had any kind of clue, we would have been found out in a split second. And what was that about chasing down communists in Hawaii?"

Finn chuckled. "It's the plot to *Big Jim McLain*."

She put a hand over her eyes and shook her head. "Let me guess. A John Wayne movie?"

Finn reached out and gave her shoulder a squeeze. "Haven't you learned that there's a Duke movie for all occasions?"

"I'm beginning to see that. They may not always be a perfect fit, but you seem to have a talent for forcing them into shape. Come on, let's take a look at this schedule and let Penny know whats going on. She was not happy to be left in the car."

Finn started walking. "Yeah, I've seen a lot of FBI movies, and not once have they had a dragon for a partner."

"Well, Bruce Lee played an agent in a movie called *Enter the Dragon*, but that's about as close as I can get," Mila said, opening the door to the Hellcat.

"Shir?" Penny asked. The box of Charleston Chews they had left with her sat empty in the cupholder.

"Yup. We got it." Mila shook the papers in her hand. "It was easier than I thought it was going to be."

Finn climbed into the passenger seat and took the schedule when Mila handed it to him, so she could start the car. Penny climbed onto Finn's shoulder and read along with him.

"It says here she's in the Engineering School," Finn commented.

"Chi. Squee, shir." Penny pointed halfway down the schedule.

"Oh, yeah. That's in fifteen minutes," Finn said, checking the clock on the dash.

"What is?" Mila asked, pulling out of the parking lot and onto the access road.

"She has a Calculus IV class in a few minutes, and she's coming from a lab across campus." Finn pulled up the map of the university Penny had found online. "If we go sit in this outdoor area, we'll be able to see her walking between buildings."

"We still don't know what she looks like," Mila argued. "Not really."

"Her student ID photo is in here." He held up the papers, showing the grainy photo.

Mila glanced at the image then the map when they stopped at a stop sign. "It's not a very good photo, but it'll do. I think I can park in the lot over there." She turned on her signal and took a right. Three minutes later, they were walking towards the area Finn had pointed out.

"Stay in the hammock, Penny. I have a feeling you would draw a crowd of gawkers. Probably try to snatch you up and take you to a lab or something." Finn joked, spotting eye rolls form both Penny and Mila, but she did climb into the mesh hammock under his jacket.

"We should use a concealment for Penny. That way, she could come out in public more."

Finn shook his head, a stern look on his face. "You can't say that." He whispered. "Dragons are far too proud to have their looks concealed. That would be like me asking you to put on clown makeup when you go out."

"Well, if I was infiltrating a gang of clowns..." Mila shrugged, letting the rest go unsaid.

"Shir chi." Pennys muffled voice said.

Mila chuckled. "Okay. I get it. No need to call me a clown. My everyday makeup isn't that heavy."

# CHAPTER FOURTEEN

F inn found them a bench under a large tree that had kept most of the snow off the seat. After brushing off what was left, he and Mila sat down. Penny climbed out of her hammock and sat beside Finn. He kept his jacket over her, so she stayed out of sight.

Classes were going, so the area was relatively empty, save for a few small groups moving between buildings. Finn began scanning the groups but didn't see any read heads. In fact, he was having trouble seeing any hair.

"This might be harder than I thought. Everyone has a hat on." Finn said, reaching for his Charleston Chews, only to realize that Penny ate them all in the car.

"Well, it is winter. People tend to wear hats this time of year."

Finn grumped at not having his candies on hand. "Well, it's damn inconvenient."

Mila laughed. "Not if you have cold ears. Speaking of which, I need to get a hat myself. Especially if we're going to be sitting outside a lot. My Mexican blood is complaining louder than my Idaho blood." She cupped her fingers over her nose to keep it from freezing off.

"It's not even that cold."

She scooted closer to him for warmth. "Said like a true four hundred pound person. You produce more heat than our whole condo."

"Plus, we dwarves handle hot and cold temperatures better than most."

"So you keep reminding me." She said, worming her way under his arm. "I think you forget just how little meat I have on my bones."

He squeezed her close. "You have enough meat for me."

"Such a charmer." She laughed. "I think it's about time."

The doors to several buildings crowded as groups of students piled out.

Finn focused on faces, still scanning for red hair, but there were so many students he was having trouble differentiating them.

Mila narrowed her eyes but kept her hands cupped over her nose. "I don't see her. There are so many people."

Penny chuckled, looking at the two of them like they were blind, and pointed. "Shir? Chi chi."

Finn and Mila followed the talon and immediately spotted Stephanie. She wasn't even wearing a hat, her bright red curls shining in the afternoon sun like a beacon.

"Oh, right. I see her," Finn said. "No need to ask how my eyes are doing."

"Chi?"

"Yes, I'm sure." He chuckled. "Man, you're a jerk sometimes."

"She's our jerk, though, and I wouldn't want it any other

way," Mila said, reaching across Finn and giving Penny a fist bump.

"So, how do we do this?" Finn asked, getting down to business. "It looks like she's with half a dozen other girls. Do we just go up and pull her to the side?"

Mila pulled the runic paper from her jacket pocket. "Sure. We have badges and everything."

"Let's hang back a second. I want to see if I can detect any magic coming from her," Finn said, opening himself up so he could see her aura.

As soon as his vision changed ever so slightly, he lost sight of Stephanie. He blinked and returned his view to normal, and she was there again. He switched back and forth, but to Finn's shock, she didn't have an aura at all.

"How is that even possible?" he muttered.

"How is what possible?" Mila asked, watching the attractive young woman walk across the brick walkway with her friends.

"She doesn't have an aura."

"So, she doesn't have access to her magic?" Mila guessed.

Finn shook his head. "No, even a Peabrain that hasn't awoken has an aura. Everyone has one. I think hers is being hidden on purpose."

Penny pointed to the side, poking Finn to get his attention. "Squee."

Finn glanced over and saw a tall man in a long black wool coat, flanked by five men and women dressed in campus police uniforms.

"Shit," Finn grumbled. "The fun police."

"I'm pretty sure they're the regular police," Mila

quipped, standing along with Finn as the group approached.

"Shir shee. Squee chi," Penny whispered as she dug into Finn's pocket and pulled out a quarter before scurrying off the bench and up the tree behind them.

"Penny wants us to keep them busy for a minute," Finn said out of the side of his mouth.

"Why?" Mila said back, her lips not moving.

"She's going to put a tracker on Stephanie," was all he could say before the group was upon them.

The man in the overcoat had an angry look on his face that only got worse when he saw the two of them whispering to one another.

"You two. Stop right there." He shouted, a little too loudly for as close as they were.

Several of the students noticed the exchange and, in true young person fashion, stopped to watch. Finn glanced to the side and saw that Stephanie was one of them, but he also caught the blue glimmer of Penny flying high overhead.

"What can we do for you…" Finn let the question linger.

"Dean Gurtz." The tall coated man said, brushing back a head full of black hair. "And, who may I ask are you? Because your FBI story didn't check out. They don't seem to know you from Adam. My assistant told me you stole a student's file earlier. I will need that back immediately."

"I'm sorry, Gretchen told you we stole the file?" Finn asked, his eyebrow raised. "She printed it out for us. We showed her our badges and everything." Finn pulled out his 'badge' and flipped it open for the Dean to see.

The man cocked an eyebrow looking from the paper to Finn. "That is just a piece of paper with some runes drawn on. I don't suppose you have a real badge in that ratty coat?"

Finn blinked, looking at the paper in his hand. It had never not worked before. He held the paper up to his face and stared at it. The runes should have been glowing purple with his power, but they had a slight green tinge to them.

Stuffing the paper in his pocket, he glanced at the group of police behind the dean and was shocked to see that two of them were elves, their ears on display poking up past their black caps. The other three looked human, but he quickly saw their auras come into focus and noted that two of them were Kashgar, and the third was a witch.

Finn sniffed and smelled the taint of dark magic all over them.

"We're sorry that the main office didn't corroborate our story," Mila stepped forward, speaking when Finn didn't respond, "but you know how it is with agents in the field. We have to keep things secret. It's our job."

Finn narrowed his eyes and saw that the dean was not what he appeared either. Finn had no idea how he had missed it at first, but this man was clearly a Kashgar, and he was mired in dark magic. It clung to him so thickly Finn felt like he could reach out and wipe some off with a finger. How had he missed this?

Glancing over towards Stephanie, who was staying at the edge of the crowd, Finn noticed Penny walking towards the young woman. The small dragon stumbled once, but leaped up onto Stephanie's backpack and dropped a coin into one of the pockets. Penny blinked a few times, then retreated to the bricks and ran for everything she had towards the parking lot.

Why wasn't she flying? And Finn had only ever seen her stumble when she was drunk (not on alcohol; dragons can't get drunk on spirits) and only when she had been on a bender when they first met while trying to drown her sorrows. That stumble was more concerning than the fact that the dean was obviously in the employ of Hellena.

Finn's eyes went wide, and he snapped his head back around to see that Mila and the dean were starting to argue in earnest. Finn interrupted by holding out the schedule to the dean.

"Here." Finn nearly threw the papers at him. "We're sorry the head office was giving you trouble. We have what we need. Thank you. Come on, Agent Vallon. We need to go."

To Mila's credit, she didn't even argue, just turned and followed Finn closely. The crowd of students seemed disappointed that nothing more was going to happen, and the dean and his people were all slightly slack-jawed at the turnaround.

"What the hell was that?" Mila asked, making a point not to turn around.

"You know how magic is getting all twisted?"

She nodded. "Yeah. Oh, my god. Is that why they dropped their concealment spells? I thought they were trying to intimidate us or something."

Finn shook his head. "Nope. Magic was all fucked up back there. It's why my paper didn't work, and I think Penny lost her ability to fly. Not to mention the dean and his cronies stunk of the Dark Star's magic. They were her people."

Mila frowned. "She sent a fake dean over to drive us away?"

"I don't think so. I think Hellena has the actual dean on her payroll. Probably has him looking out for Stephanie. He never called the FBI. If he had, Preston's people would have told him we were legit. This woman has her fingers deep in this school."

They came to the car and found Penny on the hood, her eyes a little glassy.

"You okay?" Finn asked, leaning down and lifting her chin so he could look into her eyes.

"Chi," Penny said, a smoke ring rising from a nostril.

"Did you lose control of your magic?" Mila asked, unlocking the car and opening the door.

Penny nodded. "Shir. Chi squee." She held up her arms, and Finn picked her up like a child, carrying her around to the passenger side.

"I bet it was scary," Finn said, patting her back. "You're practically all magic. That could have been really dangerous for you."

They climbed in, and Mila started the car, pulling out of the space and heading for the exit.

"I think we have a tail," Mila said, looking in the rearview mirror.

Finn turned to see a campus police car tailing them. "Just get us off-campus. They won't be able to do much once we leave."

Mila stepped on it, taking the curved road out to the main streets at speed, making the tail have to cut someone off to get out of the parking lot in time. By the time he caught up with them, Mila had them headed down the main drag out of town.

She was so focused on the cop behind them, Mila nearly hit a jacked-up black truck that pulled out in front of her. She swerved and passed in the left lane.

"What the fuck? Don't people know how to drive around here?" She shouted, looking to see that the first truck had been joined by a second identical black truck. A third pulled out from a side street to join the convoy.

"Fuck. I think we have a new tail," she said, her eyes wide.

"Just be cool. We can still get out of here without a fight."

The dragon snapped her neck to the side, making it crack all the way up. She smiled and gave a thumbs up.

"That is so gross," Finn said, a look of disgust on his face. "You know I hate when you do that."

Penny just shrugged.

Mila pulled up to a stoplight, still watching the trucks as they slowly changed lanes so that one was to either side and one behind them.

"I don't like the look of this, Finn."

The truck on the driver's side pulled up, and they could see the passenger was wearing the same black fatigues the Dark Star's men had at the lake house. Finn glanced over to his side, and it was more of the same. He glanced past the truck and saw two more trucks barreling down the side street they were stopped at, obviously going to try and box them in.

"Hey, Mila. You know how I said play it cool?"

"Yeah."

"I was wrong. Get us the fuck out of here." He pointed at the incoming trucks.

"Oh, fuck yeah. I always wanted an excuse to use the Cat in a car chase. Life has gotten so much better now that you and Penny are here." Mila had an evil grin on her face.

She dropped the Hellcat into sport shifting mode and floored it. The engine roared, spinning the tires while the traction control tried to compensate for all 700 plus horsepower going to the back wheels. After a second, the black Challenger rocketed out of its own tire smoke, running the red light, and passing the two incoming trucks well before they had a chance to block it in.

To Finn's horror, Mila's shouted, "Wahooo!" was barely audible over the screaming engine.

## CHAPTER FIFTEEN

The heavy Hellcat danced between slower-moving cars, rocking on its stiff chassis, trying to keep the weight evenly distributed as the engine poured on the speed.

Finn's knuckles were white where he gripped the center console and door handle tight enough he was afraid he might crush them. Penny was pinned to his chest in the violent acceleration and had her mouth open wide as she panted with fear. Mila was having the time of her life.

In all their time together, Finn had thought Mila was pushing herself with her aggressive driving. Turns out, he couldn't have been further from the truth. She had been holding back. If the last thirty seconds was any indication, she had been holding back a lot.

He glanced over and saw nothing but focused determination on her face as she slapped the shifter up and down to get that bit of extra out of the high-performance car. She was like a hawk eying her prey, nothing could break that concentration. Finn happened to look at the dash, and instantly regretted it when he saw that they were doing nearly a hundred and twenty, and hadn't even gotten entirely out of the city.

Glancing behind them, Finn was shocked to see three of the trucks were keeping up with them. After a second, Finn realized it was because Mila had to clear the traffic ahead of them, while all the trucks had to do was follow.

The last light before the road became a two-lane highway into the mountains flashed by while it was turning red, but Mila had crossed the intersection so fast that no one had had a chance to even begin to accelerate. The trucks coming in behind them, however, were not as lucky. Finn could see what was about to happen. Traffic would pull out and the vehicles would hit them, ending the chase, but also, more than likely, end the bystanders' lives as well.

"Fuck," Finn growled, focusing his magic.

He gritted his teeth and expelled a large amount of magic while whispering, "*Bòrd.*"

The cabin of the Hellcat filled with the smell of pine, and Finn felt his power rush out in a sucking motion, draining him for a second.

The ground beneath the lead cars in the intersection was suddenly lifted in square table-like chunks. Cars were suspended by the undercarriage on asphalt and stone slabs that left the wheels spinning in the open air. The move left the people safe, if a little confused, but that meant the chase was far from over for Mila.

She downshifted as the grade of the road increased, climbing up into the mountains to the west of town. She passed a Subaru, drifting the car around a tight switchback, rocketing out of the turn, just to have to do the same maneuver going the opposite way a few seconds later.

Finn bit his tongue just to keep from shouting for her to look out. She obviously saw the cars ahead of her and had a plan to get around them, even if he had no clue what that plan was.

"I kinda wish that spell you put on the tires when we went up to the lake hadn't worn off. It would make this all a lot easier," Mila said as she had to go onto the slim berm, spitting rocks down onto the road below.

Finn felt his asshole tighten so much he thought he wouldn't be able to shit for a week as he stared down the mountainside. Seeing the trucks racing to keep up a few turns below made Finn begrudgingly have to give the drivers credit for keeping up as well as they had.

"Shit," Mila said calmly.

That one word made Finn go white. He glanced at the traffic stopped ahead due to some jam further up the mountain.

"I see a firebreak road. I think I can get to it before oncoming traffic cuts us off." She pushed the accelerator to the floor, making the car's back tires rumble as they broke free for a second, even though they were already doing sixty.

She swerved into the oncoming lane with a semi coming down the mountain right at them. The car sped up to over a hundred in a few seconds, the whole thing hunkering close to the road as the speed increased.

Finn wasn't breathing.

The semi laid on the horn, locking up its brakes. White

smoke billowed out from the wheels, and the rig bounced as it fought to slow its forward momentum.

They rushed towards the truck, and all Finn could focus on was the chrome grill, thinking of how he was going to be nothing but ground meat in a second. Then Mila slammed on the breaks, making him and Penny fly forward, only the seatbelt and Finn's quick reactions allowing him to snatch her from the air before she slammed into the dash. The car squealed as it went from trying to go as fast as possible to stopping in the span of a millisecond.

The truck barreled down on them. At the last second, Mila spun the wheel, and they dropped off the highway and onto a snow-covered, gravel-packed road. The semi flew past where they had been moments before.

Rocks and pebbles slammed into the bottom of the Hellcat like a drummer on every drug ever made at the same time while trying to break the world speed record for the fastest drum roll. Even the thought of conversation seemed impossible in the sudden cacophony.

Finn peered out the back window and was shocked to see that the trucks were turning onto the fire road. They must have used their off-road capabilities to get past the semi entirely blocking the road now that it had stopped. They were a good half mile or more ahead of their pursuers, but the way the car slid back and forth at the slightest incline meant they had to slow down, while the trucks' four-by-four drive trains were coping with the loose gravel just fine.

"Uh, I don't mean to be a bother, but do you know where this road goes?" Finn asked as calmly as he could. He stared past Mila and down the very close edge of the road. It was a long way down before they would stop if she happened to go over the edge.

"No idea. These firebreaks meet up with other main roads." She slid them around a corner, the back tire shooting rocks and snow out into the open air behind them. "Usually."

Finn nodded. She was doing the best she could. He watched the corner they had gone around, counting out the time it took before the first truck was visible. They rounded another corner, and he did the same thing. The time was shorter. Not much, but it was a few seconds. They were catching up. If they could get through this and find another main road, then he was sure Mila could lose them. They just had to stay ahead.

An idea came to Finn. He was a little drained from earlier, but they were surrounded by rock. Finn could work with that. He closed his eyes and focused on the loose rock in the upper hills. He envisioned it rumbling along with the sound of the engine, shaking free, and tumbling into more rock further down, and so on. Then, he envisioned a rock slide. Finn began to power the spell.

He was thrown against the seatbelt, the wind knocked out of him. His eyes snapped open, and he saw they were sliding towards a downed tree blocking the road. Finn guessed it was a good two feet thick, far to thick to drive through, and more than likely too heavy to move.

The car stopped two feet from the massive tree, the engine purring with anticipation, but with nowhere to go.

"Fuck," Mila said, looking for a way around the tree.

"Damn it! I was having a blast. Now we have to fight these fuckers." She shut the car off with a pout.

Finn and Penny stared at her for a long second.

"What?" she asked. "I like to drive. I haven't had that much fun driving in years."

Finn laughed. "You are amazing."

She smirked, pulling the Ivar pistol from the small of her back. "I know."

---

Finn stepped out of the car, reached around under his jacket, and pulled Fragar free. He whispered the power word and the ax unfolded in a flash. He looked over and saw Mila doing the same with her armor, only the high collar of the chainmail visible as it formed over her skin. Gram was in her off-hand a second later, the gleaming golden blade humming with power.

Finn set his feet as the roar of multiple engines signaled the trucks were cornering the last bend. He watched as they slid to a halt, the engines shutting off and two guys getting out of each of the five vehicles.

The sudden silence on the side of the mountain was only interrupted by the loud pinging of rapidly cooling metal as the taxed engines sat in the frigid air.

The black-clad soldiers approached cautiously, no visible weapons on their persons. That made Finn more nervous than if they were all carrying guns. No guns meant that the men themselves were weapons, and upon closer inspection, he could see they were all Kashgar, and therefore adept at magic.

One of the men stepped closer than the rest, staring at the two of them with contempt. "You know, I hate having to chase people. It's so annoying. And look what it got you?" he waved a hand out over the open expanse looking down on Boulder. "At least you die with a pleasing view."

"You work for the Dark Star," Finn said, raising an eyebrow. "We have a deal with her. She said she was going to hunt us down herself. If I were you, I wouldn't do anything to piss her off, like kill us without her present."

The tall man scratched at his bald head. "Yeah, the thing is, we all know about that. And if it were any other circumstance, you'd be right." He licked his teeth, making a sucking sound. "But there is one thing she won't stand for. You fucked with her daughter." He shook a finger at them. "That's a big no-no."

Finn cocked his head and looked over at Mila. "This guy's a little over the top."

She gave a shrug.

"I mean, I'm not crazy here, right?" he pointed Fragar at the bald man. "He just sucked his teeth at us." Finn turned back to the man and furrowed his brow. "Tell me the truth, you practiced that speech in the mirror, didn't you?"

The other nine guys chuckled, but a dark look from their leader silenced them. His face was red when he turned back to face Finn and Mila, but Finn couldn't tell if it was from embarrassment or anger.

"Look, we didn't really know if Stephanie was her daughter or not. Now that we do, we can leave her alone. We don't have to fight, and you all don't have to die." Finn shrugged, looking up to his shoulder to give Penny a smirk. She always liked it when he said clever things, but she wasn't there.

Finn frowned and looked over to Mila, expecting Penny to be with her, but her shoulders were empty.

"There are ten of us, and two of you. In what world do you two walk away from this?" the leader said, holding up his hand and forming a small bubble that filled with swirling fire.

"Well," Finn's attention was dragged back to the problem at hand, "I would say pretty much all of them. You think I could go around the galaxy talking the kind of shit I do without having been in a few five-on-one fights?"

The leader made a face like he had eaten a lemon. "It's ten-to-two, you moron. Not five on one. I'll give you some credit and maybe concede that you could take out five guys, but you don't stand a chance against twice that."

Finn blinked in confusion. "Huh? That's what I said. It's five-to-one odds here, bub." He looked over at Mila, but she looked just as confused.

Now it was the bald guy giving them an incredulous stare. "You must be the dumbest dwarf in the galaxy. I just told you there are ten of us. Can't you count?"

"Uh, boss." One of the younger guys stepped forward, missing the look on his partner's face that said to keep his mouth shut. "I think he's talking ratio. Like five to one is the same as—"

"Shut the fuck up, Jeffrey!" The bald guy screamed, a vein throbbing on his forehead. "Just shut. The fuck. Up." He glared at the man until the soldier took a step back into line. The leader turned to Finn, his face a mask of rage. "The fact that you know the daughter even exists makes you a liability. Our lord doesn't abide by liabilities. Your sentence is death."

Finn puffed out his cheeks in a long exhale. "Boy, oh, boy. If she doesn't abide by liabilities, you better pray no one reports your abysmal grasp of fractions. That's a pretty big liability all on its own, but your inability to take criticism on the matter is just... fuck man; that's just dangerous."

Finn would have sworn he could see steam coming off of baldy's head. When Mila started laughing softly, it about caused an aneurysm.

"Kill these motherfuckers!" the guy screamed, throwing his premade fireball.

Finn and Mila dove away from one another, letting the bubble fly between them, expecting a flaming explosion. However, when no explosion came, Finn glanced over to where a burning crater should be and saw a splash of orange color in the snow as if someone had thrown a bucket of paint.

The attackers all had bubbles up at this point, so Finn wrote it off as the bald guy getting too worked up to properly use his magic.

Finn pushed off the ground with his back foot, raking his free hand into the snow and scooping up a handful of rocks along with it, charged the guys on the right.

They raised their hands, looks of concentration, and only a little fear on their faces. They let the spells fly. Finn held up Fragar as a shield and smacked the first bubble away before it could fully form. The second bubble popped and a large bouquet of flowers snapped into reality as Finn ducked to the right, letting the flowers fly over his head.

Finn whipped his hand up, focusing a chunk of his magic into it and shouting, *"Leaghadh!"* before throwing the handful of rocks and snow at the two men.

The snow vaporized into steam as the rocks glowed with heat. They turned to magma and splashed across three men. Their jackets burst into flame as the liquid rock hit them, making two of the men run and the third to drop to the ground and roll around.

A bolt of white energy from Mila's Ivar pistol shot the top half of one of the Kashgar off before it slammed into the second truck in the line, making it explode, and cartwheel over the cliff.

Finn realized just about the same time that the Kashgar did that their magic was not doing what they wanted it to. Everyone stopped. Finn felt terrible about killing helpless men, so he backed away. They did the same. He held a hand up for Mila to let them go.

The Kashgar got back to the lead truck and, all at once, piled into the back. Finn cocked his head and looked at Mila, who shrugged.

"Why are they getting in the back... oh, fuck." Finn's question was answered when baldy stood up in the bed of the truck and leveled an RPG at him.

"Have some Peabrain magic, you fucking—"

The truck exploded as another bolt from the Ivar slammed into it. The rocket-propelled grenade shot up into the air as the truck and the remaining six Kashgar were tossed into the air.

Finn watched the grenade shuttle up and veer towards the snow-covered mountain peak. His face dropped when he saw what was about to happen.

The truck landed on the road, the front half blown off, and Kashgar fell all around it, along with the contents of the truck, which happened to be a small arsenal.

Finn ignored them, including the groans of pain from those that had survived the first blast and the fall back to earth. He turned and focused on the tree blocking their path. Finn took a knee as the sound of the grenade exploding high above them thumped through the valley.

Digging his hand down until he felt rock, he channeled magic into the ground. "*Colbh cloiche!*"

A stone column shot up into the air under the root end of the tree, launching the massive thing into the air. The tree spun into the valley below.

"We need to go now!" Finn shouted.

She was staring, not at the tumbling tree or the massive two-foot thick column of stone, but up the mountain's slope where the grenade had broken loose several weeks' of built-up snow.

"Mila!" he shouted, snapping her out of her daze.

She did a double-take as she saw the tree was gone, and their path was clear.

"Right! Where's Penny?" Mila shouted over the intensifying rumble.

Finn opened the passenger side door and saw Penny lying unconscious on the seat. "She's here. We need to get the fuck out of here. You wanted more driving, well, here's your chance, darlin'."

Mila snapped out of her daze at the mention of more driving. She hopped into the car and had it started and throwing snow and gravel out behind them before her door was even shut.

## CHAPTER SIXTEEN

Mila raced along the firebreak road, not taking the time to check the rearview mirror. Either they would make it, or they wouldn't, and her checking was just a distraction. She turned the wheel, letting off the gas as they approached a tight turn, and the car rumbled. She had noticed the vibrations when she had the pedal down, but she thought it was the engine. Now that the car was taking a breather, she realized it wasn't the vehicle shaking, but the mountain.

Sliding into the corner, Mila feathered the gas, keeping just enough power to take the turn at speed, but not so much they risked spinning out.

She could see where the road would turn back to the right, getting them out of the depression the avalanche was racing down, but it was still a few seconds away, and the car was now beginning to bounce as millions of tons of snow cannonballed along down the mountain, shaking the very stones of the earth.

Mila chanced a quick look in the mirror and saw the

leading edge of the avalanche smash into the road, shoving the remaining black trucks over the side.

Mila swallowed and pushed the pedal down more. Snow and rock slammed into the road behind them, catching up to the speeding Hellcat.

"We're not going to make it."

"We're going to make it. Just focus," Finn said in a calm voice as he cradled the unconscious Penny.

Mila leaned forward, gripping the steering wheel so tight the leather squeaked under her sweaty palms. She couldn't help but catch a glimpse of the white torrent of death closing in. She gave the car more gas.

The turn came faster than anticipated, while at the same time taking forever. Mila slammed on the brakes and turned the wheel right, sending the car into a sideways slide. She stomped on the gas while the blurring cliffside filled the windscreen. Wheels spinning, they chewed into the snow and loose gravel, adding an insignificant amount to the river of snow and rock tumbling down the mountain behind them.

Traction control kicked in and launched them forward towards the cliff face, but their sideways momentum slid them around the corner just in time to rocket down the road.

Mila breathed a sigh of relief as she slowed down and glanced in the rearview mirror. From around the sharp turn, she could see the avalanche plowing through the dense tree cover, ripping them from the mountain and adding their weight to the wave of death.

A *crack* and a *pop* made Mila snap her head over to see Finn releasing the folding handhold above the door. Her jaw dropped when she saw that he had crushed the leather-covered plastic handle into a twisted wreck.

"Dude." She shouted, pointing at the handhold. "Careful with my baby. Do you know how much that's going to cost to fix?"

Finn raised an eyebrow. "I'm not taking credit for that. You did something that no one in the universe has ever done. You made me vomit from motion sickness. I swallowed it, but the cost of not having me spew my breakfast all over the place is a broken handle. Besides, I can repair it with a spell. The more important thing we need to deal with is Penny." He held her limp form up so Mila could see it.

She had heard him say Penny was out and even saw her in his hands, but it hadn't really hit her what that meant.

Mila's jaw dropped. "What the fuck happened? Did she get hurt in the fight?"

Finn shook his head. "I think whatever has been messing with magic is happening to her. She was feeling woozy in town, but she seemed to be recovering before we got into the chase. We need to get away from the area of effect of whatever this is." He held her body up to his ear as he listened to her heartbeat. "We need to hurry. Her heart is weak. I hate to say this, but step on it."

Mila nodded and picked up speed. She didn't go as fast and reckless as on her way up the mountain, but she still pushed the limits.

Taking only the occasional glance at Finn and Penny, Mila got to see an interesting side to their relationship.

Finn's face was stony, but with a slight downturn to his lips, as he watched for any sign of change in his friend. She noticed he was absent-mindedly stroking her wing, and occasionally he would mutter some vague promise to her if she would just wake up. Mila had made promises like that in her times of dire need; everyone had.

A sniff from Finn made Mila take her eyes from the road and glance at him. Tears wet his cheeks, but he made no move to wipe them away.

Mila reached over and stroked Penny's hip, the only thing she could reach as Finn cradled her against his chest. "She's going to be okay. If we get to town and she's still not up, we keep on going until she does. We'll keep her safe."

Finn nodded, not taking his eyes off of her. "I know we will. But this is bad. Dragons are mostly solidified magic, they don't have a whole lot of biological parts to them, especially faerie dragons." He sniffed. "I promised I would keep her safe while we found her a hoard." He choked out a laugh. "Stupid little jerk never even told me what we were looking for. She just stuck with me while I fumbled our way through the universe. Whenever we found an artifact or some lost treasure, I would ask if it was what she needed. She would just shake her head and laugh."

"She does that shit to me too, you know. She's been your partner for a long time, and it's hard to see your friends in a bad way, but she's going to be fine."

Finn shook his head. "She hasn't been my partner for a long time. Twenty years ago, she got her wings broken, saving my sorry ass during a fight with a pack of rat-men. Since that day we've been family. I'm the only one she's got, and she's the only one I've got."

Mila saw the end of the firebreak road and a paved highway that led down into Boulder. "Not anymore. I know you guys have history, but no matter how you slice it, there are three of us now. It's not you and Penny against the universe. Now it's the three of us." She smiled at him, her heart breaking to see the big dwarf so distraught. "Three might not seem like much, but its fifty percent more than when you got here."

Finn gave her a half-smile and nodded."I know you're with us. Penny does too. Don't tell her I said this, but she told me you're her favorite person she's ever met."

Mila felt her cheeks flush. "That's sweet." She said, slowing the car to a stop and pulling onto the highway, then laying on some speed to get them away from the mountain and its twisted magic.

"You don't understand." Finn pressed, patting Penny on the side. "Penny is over two hundred and fifty years old. Do you know how many people you meet in two hundred and fifty years?"

Mila looked over at the tiny dragon, her mouth open in shock. How could she be that old? She was so...snarky. A memory of Mila's *abuela* flashed in her mind, and she realized Penny wasn't some rebellious young teen like her snarky attitude suggested; she was an old woman who was done with everyone's shit. The thought almost made her laugh, but she controlled herself.

"I'm guessing it's a lot of people?" Mila said, with a shrug.

Finn nodded. "Yeah. It's a lot. And, of all those people, you are her favorite. That's the nicest thing I've heard her say about anyone. Including me."

Penny sucked in a breath and shot up into a sitting position in Finn's arms. She coughed a gassy plume of flame that shot out, making Mila duck or have her hair burned off.

The car swerved as Mila dove towards the shifter to get out of the fireball's way. A car horn made Mila jerk the wheel the other way. She popped them back up and found their lane, waving an apology at the car next to them.

Finn rolled the window down and turned Penny, so she was facing away from Mila, and towards the car next to them. Mila saw that the guy was giving her the finger for nearly hitting him, but his expression changed when Penny started coughing balls of flame at him. Mila didn't see much of his face past the yellow and orange coughing fit, but she did see his car back off and leave them a wide berth.

After a minute, Penny calmed, and Finn rolled the window up.

"You okay?" Finn asked, wiping any residual wetness from his face. "You scared the shit out of us."

Penny climbed into his lap and shook out her scales before flexing her wings a few times. She sat on his knee, her eyes a little bleary as she blinked. She gazed at him and puffed a smoke ring from her nostrils.

Finn smiled. "We need to do something about that. Can't have you going to Lala land every time we come across whatever this is. I'm going to send a message to Hermin and Garret. Maybe they'll have an idea."

Penny nodded, deep in thought.

"Do you need something?" Mila asked, concern in her voice.

Penny looked at her, and the corner of her mouth went up in a half-smile. "Chi. Shir." She pointed at her stomach.

Mila laughed. "We can do that. I could use some lunch myself after using the Ivar twice." She stepped on the gas and sped down the mountain towards a good lunch.

They rode in silence for a minute, then Mila raised an eyebrow and looked over at Finn. "You said you two have been partners for twenty years?"

"More than twenty. It was twenty years when I realized we were family." Finn said, eliciting a smile from Penny.

"How long have you been together?" Mila asked, a suspicion rising.

Finn and Penny communicated silently the way long time partners do. "About thirty years or so. Right?"

"Shir chi." Penny stated.

Finn's brows went up. "Really? Huh. I guess it's been thirty-six."

Mila licked her lips. "So, you two have been working together for thirty-six years, and you were already a treasure hunting before you met Penny. You were also in your father's army for a few years before you left home... Uh, Finn. How old are you?"

Finn looked at the ceiling doing the math in his head. He opened his mouth to answer, but Mila held up a hand and stopped him.

"You know what?" Mila shook her head. "Let's just keep it a mystery. I'm not sure I want to know, for sure, that I'm dating a geriatric."

Finn laughed. "Age is relative. Comparing our two races' rates of aging, we're about the same age."

"Oh, god. That sounds just like what a creepy old dude at a bar would say while hitting on a college girl."

Penny chuckled. "Squee, shir."

Mila burst out laughing. "You mean like a male cougar?"

Finn furrowed his brow. "What's a cougar?"

Mila laughed even harder. "It's an older woman who sleeps with young men. It's a perfect nickname!"

"No." Finn shook his head, frowning at Penny. "That is not a good nickname."

"Whatever you say, *manther*!"

Mila nearly peed herself with laughter, especially when she saw the look of defeat on Finn's face.

# CHAPTER SEVENTEEN

D riving at a reasonable pace, at least for Mila, it took twenty minutes to get to town. On the ride down the mountain, Finn sent one of the cards Hermin had given them off with a burst of magic, saying they needed to meet. Finn had written the name of the diner they had eaten at earlier since he didn't know the name of anywhere else in Boulder.

Finn made sure that Penny was actually feeling better and not just pretending to keep them from worrying. When she finally growled at him, "are you sure you're fine?" he knew she was on the mend for real.

They pulled into the diner's small lot and saw Hermin and Garret sitting in a booth by the window, both of them stuffing pancakes into their mouths.

"Looks like they didn't waste any time," Finn said, impressed Garret got the whole pancake in his mouth in one bite.

Finn climbed out of the car, Penny jumping to his

shoulder, and headed for the diner's door, holding it open for Mila. "After you, darlin'."

"Aw. Thanks, manther," she said with a wicked smile.

Finn rolled his eyes, hoping the awful nickname would go away on its own. Penny laughing hysterically on his shoulder made him think he might have to come up with a new tactic.

"Oh, you two are hilarious," Finn grumped, following Mila into the old-timey diner filled with red pleather seating and chrome everything else.

Hermin was facing the door and gave them a wave when they came in. "Over here."

The two Huldu scooted over to make room in the booth, and Finn and Mila took the offered seats. Penny hopped off Finn's shoulder and snatched a piece of bacon from Garret's plate.

"Hey!" he reached out to take the bacon back, but the growl Penny let out made him think again. "Okay, I'll just order some more. No need to be rude."

"You'll have to forgive her," Mila said in Penny's defense. "She was just about dead half an hour ago. She needs to replenish her magic."

"Almost dead? What happened?" Hermin asked, stuffing another half a pancake in his mouth, dripping syrup down the corner of his beard.

"Uh, you have a little…" Mila pointed to the corner of her mouth, then slowly ran her finger towards her chin. "On second thought, you're probably going to need to wash that out."

Garret waggled a finger, and a thin stream of bubbles shot out and embedded themselves in Hermin's beard, greedily sucking up the syrup before popping away to nothing.

"Well, that's handy," Finn said, envy rearing its ugly head. "I wish I knew that little trick."

"A little anti-syrup spell I worked up about, oh...when was syrup invented?" Garret said. "Anyway, Penny was almost dead? What happened?"

Finn told the tale of the chase up the mountain and the subsequent fight and avalanche, then relayed the part about Penny being unconscious when they got back to the car.

"Oh, that avalanche was you?" Hermin sighed with relief. "I thought we had royally messed something up. Do you know how hard it is to get snow to stick to the side of a mountain? I heard it nearly drove the architects crazy trying to get it right."

"Yeah," Mila rolled her eyes, "the avalanche was us, but the fucked-up magic wasn't. We need to figure out how to stop it, or at least keep it from killing Penny."

Finn cut in, "Have you guys been affected by the twists?"

"The twists?" Hermin said, considering the phrase. "I like that, fitting name. And no, we haven't. Not really. We spoke with Preston and his people this morning, and they asked us pretty much the same thing. Honestly, we spend our days underground. I haven't noticed a thing, but a few of our people came back complaining about their magic being a little slow to react."

"Last we had heard," Garret continued, swallowing a bite of hash browns, "the effects were pretty mild. Most people have been saying that either their magic was slow, or it was harder to concentrate when casting. We haven't heard anything about it being so bad magicals are being knocked out. You okay?" he asked Penny, who sagged her shoulders in annoyance and nodded, taking a second piece of bacon.

"Penny's a little more magical than most, being a dragon and all," Finn said.

"That's true," Garret said. "I hadn't considered that. If she was knocked out, how was it when you cast?"

Finn shrugged. "I couldn't tell there was anything wrong. I don't think it affects me like it does most people. Mila was able to channel her powers through her pistol without issue."

"Yeah, I didn't notice anything, but then again, I wouldn't know what to look for. I haven't exactly been using magic. At least not in a spellcasting capacity," Mila admitted.

Hermin considered them for a second. "Maybe it doesn't affect dwarven magic? And using celestial magic, well, that's a whole other playbook. I wouldn't even know where to begin."

Finn shook his head. "We had a run-in with some guys earlier, and a runic paper of mine stopped working, and that was all dwarven magic."

Hermin leaned back, crossing his arms, thinking, while Garret leaned his elbows on the table and leaned in. "You're sure the runes didn't work? It wasn't something else?"

Finn tried to think of what else it could have been and nodded. "Yeah. I'm sure. I showed it to them, and they saw a piece of paper with runes on it. Now that I think about it, the runes were glowing green, not purple like they should have been."

Garret was about to say something when the waitress came to the table. It was the same woman that had served them earlier, and she recognized them; Penny in particular.

"You're back," she said, a little surprised. "You know what you want?"

Mila ordered a club sandwich and water, then her phone started ringing, and she checked the caller ID. "Huh. I need to take this," she said, excusing herself and sliding out of the booth.

Finn watched her go, but Penny's rumbling stomach brought him back to the task at hand. He ordered a French dip with fries and steak and baked potato for Penny.

The waitress lifted an eyebrow. "You're ordering your lizard a steak?"

Finn reached out and grabbed hold of Penny's tail, keeping her in place as she lunged. "She's had a rough day. She deserves it. Thanks."

The waitress shrugged and walked away to put in the order.

"Maybe it's because you do most of your magic through touch." Hermin got right back to the conversation.

Finn shook his head. "I cast at least one spell that didn't require me to touch the ground. I superheated some rocks that I threw at the guys. It went off without even a hiccup."

"Yeah, but you were touching the stones when you cast it; you said you threw them," Hermin argued.

"The spell doesn't happen until the stones are in the air; otherwise, I would just melt my own hand."

The two Huldu nodded and sat back to think some more.

Penny, seeing that they were not watching their plates, helped herself to Hermin's hash browns.

———

Mila hit the answer button and put the phone to her ear. "Professor Hoff... Gregory. I didn't expect to hear from you for a while."

"Mila." Gregory's voice was excited. "You are not going to believe what has happened to me!"

Mila smiled. She had never heard him so animated. "What?"

"After I left your place last night, I couldn't sleep, so I started making some calls. I've gotten quite a few contacts in the magical world over the years. I asked if they had any information on Valkyries. Most of them didn't know anything more than I shared with you. I wasn't getting anywhere, so I went to my local market. You know what kind of 'market' I'm talking about?"

Mila laughed. "Yes. I've been several times."

"Good, good. I went down to the market and asked around; in person, people were even less inclined to tell me anything. So, eventually, I went home."

Mila waited for the bomb to drop, but remembered that Gregory always liked his students to prompt him. She guessed it was his way of making sure they were engaged in the lesson.

"And?" Mila said, drawing out the word.

Mila could hear the smile in his voice. "And I got a call. From a Valkyrie."

"Seriously?!"

"Yes, dear. Seriously. At first, the Valkyrie was all threats, telling me to stop drawing attention to them, or she would have to do something about it, but when I said I had been asking around for another Valkyrie, she changed her tune." He chuckled. "Well, actually, she was still pretty intense, but she wanted to know all about you. Now, of course, I'm not just giving out your information to a stranger, so I told her she would have to leave a number, and I could have you call her. So she gave me her number, and I'm sending it to you now."

Mila's phone *dinged*, and she looked to see a text notification from Gregory. [Victoria Gara 919-476-...]

"Got it. Gregory, this is amazing. I don't know how to thank you," Mila said, unable to contain her excitement.

"No need to thank me at all, dear. I always look out for my students. But that wasn't all. She also gave me a message to pass on to you." He cleared his throat, and she heard a piece of paper crinkle on his end. "I didn't want to get this wrong, so I wrote it down. You ready?"

"Yes!"

"Okay. Victoria, that's her name, she said, 'Your power comes from who you are, not what you are. Your convictions are the catalyst, not your desire. Trust in yourself, and you will have all the control you need.' I'm not sure what she means there, but hopefully, it helps."

Mila nodded, committing the words to memory. "I think I understand. Thank you so much, Gregory. How can I repay you? Seriously."

He chuckled. "Well, if you're insisting. I hear there is a Dryad that sells tooters at your Market. If you could overnight me a few, I would be very grateful. The tooter game up here in Canada is, well, I'm not entirely sure there *are* even tooters, to tell the truth."

Mila swallowed hard, trying not to gag. "I'll see what I can do. Thanks"

"My pleasure."

Finn smiled at Mila as she sat at the table, and her face split into a smile. She unrolled her silverware and placed the napkin across her lap, before picking up one of her club sandwich corners and taking a bite.

"Good call?" Finn asked.

Mila nodded, holding a hand over her mouth. "Ereal ood." A piece of turkey fell out of her mouth, and she snatched it up off the table, stuffing it back into her mouth before Penny could get it. She chewed the rest of the bite and swallowed. "It was Gregory. He gave me the number for a Valkyrie that contacted him."

"Holy shit! That's great." Finn almost dropped his sandwich in his *au jus* from the news. "Are you going to call her?"

"I don't know. Probably. Not until we get home."

Finn raised an eyebrow, but it was Penny who spoke up, holding her steak in both hands, her chin dripping with meat juice. "Shir squee, chi chi."

"I know." Mila tried to sink into her seat more to get

away from their gazes. "I need to call. I'll do it, just don't pressure me. I need to be ready."

Penny nodded. "Chi chi," she said with understanding, before ripping a chunk of steak off with her teeth.

"What if it's your blood!" Hermin nearly shouted, a finger rising to the ceiling, as he suddenly rejoined the conversation.

"Oh, my god. Hermin, you scared the shit out of me." Mila said, pressing a fist to her heart. "What does my blood have to do with a phone call?"

Hermin looked at her like she had gone mad, but let the question go as Garret began nodding. "It could be blood. He is a royal. Mila we can explain with her celestial magic, but Finn has actual royal blood. That could be it."

Hermin frowned now that the theory was out, he didn't seem to be liking it as much.

"Why would my heritage have any sway over how magic interacts with me. That doesn't make sense," Finn said, not liking where this was going. Anything that brought his family into it was terrible as far as he was concerned.

"Well, it doesn't. Unless that was what they were trying to do," Garret admitted. "But it's the only reason I can figure."

"So, let me get this straight," Finn said, taking a bite of his *au jus*-soaked sandwich and chewing before continuing. "You're best theory is that the Dark Star is fucking up everyone's magic, including her own, and specifically making sure it doesn't affect me? That sounds insane."

The Huldu peered at one another, and Garret nodded. "Well, when you say it like that."

Finn chuckled. "Yeah, I don't think that's it, guys."

"Probably right." Hermin checked an imaginary watch, then glanced around the diner to be sure no one was looking. "Well, it looks like break time is over. Gotta get back to keeping the planet running. Thanks for lunch."

Both Hermin and Garret vanished in a shower of bubbles.

"Cheap bastards. Left us with the bill."

Mila reached over and squeezed his hand. "Babe. We're rich. A couple of pancakes aren't going to break the bank."

"It's just the principle of the thing."

"Who wants to go talk to Stephanie?" Mila said, changing the subject.

Penny raised her hand.

"May as well. It's not like she has her guard dogs anymore," Finn said, dipping his sandwich again.

## CHAPTER EIGHTEEN

Finn and Mila watched as Penny focused her magic between her small taloned hands, her eyes closed in concentration, a little bubble forming. Finn leaned in for a better look and saw images of Boulder flashing through the bubble, like a slideshow on fast forward.

They had moved to the car, sitting in the diner parking lot, the Hellcat running with the heat on while Penny tracked the quarter she had dropped in Stephanie's bag. Finn and Mila kept quiet while the small dragon worked.

After two minutes, Penny's eyes snapped open, and the image in the bubble stabilized, showing an old Victorian-style house close to downtown Boulder.

"Shee shir," Penny said, giving the address to Finn, who entered it into the navigation on his phone.

"Got it. You're sure she's still there?"

"Chi. Shir shee."

Mila put the car in drive and pulled out onto the road, heading for old town.

They wound their way through the older roads, passing

large houses that were far too fancy for a college student to afford until Mila pulled to the curb in front of the house they had seen in Penny's tracking spell.

"Man, I wish I lived in a place like this when I was in college," Mila said, leaning to peer past Finn and Penny at the huge house. "This place has to have a lot of zeros in the price. Must be nice to be the daughter of a supervillain."

Finn chuckled. "It's not as good as you might think. My father might not technically be a supervillain, but that depends on who you ask."

They watched the house for a few minutes, looking for signs of guards while Penny performed another spell to detect wards on the place. The dragon cocked her head to the side, blinking a few times as she considered what she felt. "Chi chi. Squee shee chir."

Finn frowned, and Mila pursed her lips. "I didn't quite get that."

"She said there are wards, but they're falling apart. It's like they haven't been powered in a while, or they have been twisted by all the magical fluctuations lately. She's convinced they're degraded enough they won't function anymore."

Mila frowned. "If this is her daughter, you would think Hellena would work to keep her protected."

Finn shrugged. "She might be so far into her darkness; she's not thinking straight. I wouldn't be surprised if she completely forgets Stephanie even exists from time to time."

"Dark magic twists someone enough that they can forget their own child?" Mila looked horrified.

"It can be all-consuming. Most of the time, by the end,

the user is the used; just a husk of their former selves. It's a blight that needs to be stamped out. Come on, let's introduce ourselves." Finn opened the car door and climbed out.

Mila followed, coming around the car to stand next to him. "Do you think she's a magic-user?"

Finn shook his head. "I checked her aura earlier at the school. She didn't have one. That means either, somehow, she's one of the rare creatures that have no magic whatsoever or, more likely, her abilities are being forcefully repressed."

"What does that mean? Besides the obvious." Mila amended.

They started up the front walk towards the door. "If I had to guess, then I would say she's a magical, but her mother blocked her abilities for some reason. Probably to keep her hidden, if I had to guess. But that means she's probably not a Peabrain."

"She looks human."

"So do I to a degree, but we both know that's not true. You would be surprised how common the human form is in the universe. It was a pretty good design, all things considered." Finn chuckled and opened his jacket. "You should probably stay out of sight, just in case she hasn't been exposed to magic at all. Don't want to start on the wrong foot."

Penny sighed. "Shir shee." She grumbled, before crawling down his chest and into the jacket.

Finn chuckled. "I agree. Non-magicals are annoying. Sorry, Penny. We gotta do what we gotta do."

They stepped up onto the wraparound porch, walking

past the white wicker furniture, and Finn knocked on the door.

They waited a full minute before Finn knocked again. "Maybe she dropped her backpack off and went somewhere?"

Mila cocked her head, listening. "No, I can hear her walking around. I think the house is just big, and it's taking her a minute to get here."

Sure enough, just as Finn was about to knock on the door again, it opened a crack, the door chain keeping the aperture just wide enough to fit her face.

Finn was surprised at how much she looked like Hellena, aside from the curling red locks spilling past her face.

"Hi. I'm agent McClain with the FBI, and this is Agent Vallon. Would you mind if we ask you a few questions?" Finn said, in a jovial voice, holding up the folded runic paper as a badge.

Stephanie looked the badge over, then looked past them, scanning the road. Her eyes narrowed as she didn't see what she was looking for. She looked between Finn and Mila, biting her lip nervously.

"One question," she said, brushing an unruly lock of curls from her face. "What are your real names? I know you don't work for the FBI. I saw you two on campus earlier when the dean ran you off."

Finn looked at Mila, his brows rising. She smirked and took the lead. "Stephanie, we need to talk. My name is Mila Winters, and this big teddy bear is Finnegan Dragonbender. We don't want to cause you any trouble, but we need to ask you a few questions about your mother."

Stephanie's eyes widened, and she again bit her lip. "My mother is dead. You can ask my dad, he lives on the other side of town."

Mila smiled. "We both know Herman isn't your father. If I had to guess, I would say you haven't even seen him in years. We need to ask you about Hellena."

Stephanie relaxed a little, again scanning the street. "They're not coming, are they?"

"The security team?" Finn shook his head. "No. They got buried in work."

Mila groaned at his terrible joke. "Do you want them to come?"

Stephanie recoiled in disgust. "God, no. Those assholes make my life miserable." She thought for a few minutes, chewing her lip. "Give me a minute, and I'll grab a coat. We can go to the coffee shop down the street. There aren't any ears listening down there."

She closed the door, and Finn looked at Mila. "Well, that was easier than I expected."

"Yeah. There is no way in hell I would go get coffee with two strangers who lied about their identities to my face. I would have called the cops."

"She could be calling them now."

"That's what I was thinking," Mila said, looking both ways down the street, making sure there wasn't a police cruiser coasting up on them.

Just when Finn was about to say they should go, the door opened, and Stephanie stepped out, pulling it closed and locking it behind her before turning to them. "Let's go."

She led the way down the steps, setting a quick pace in

the cold. Finn and Mila were forced to jog to catch up with the fast-moving young woman. She didn't say anything or even look at them as she led them two blocks to a small business district with a coffee shop situated in the center of a row of shops.

A bell rang when they opened the door, and a young woman behind the counter waved. "Hey, Steph. The usual?"

"Yeah. Thanks, Mona." Stephanie made a beeline for a booth in the back.

"What can I get you two?" the barista asked as Finn and Mila passed the counter.

"I'm good, thanks," Mila said.

"We'll have coffee," Finn said at the same time.

Stephanie slid into the booth, pulling off her puffy blue coat and white knit hat, settling into the squeaky seat.

Finn and Mila took the other side, and they stared at one another until Mona brought their drinks. They thanked her, then sipped on their coffee for a few seconds.

"Is she in trouble?" Stephanie asked, sipping on her latte in a large white cup. "Or *is* she the trouble?"

Finn liked this girl; she was sharp. "She's the trouble."

Stephanie deflated. "I thought so."

Mila leaned in. "She's also in trouble. We're trying to stop her from hurting herself and a lot of innocent people."

Stephanie sighed, her eyes misting with tears. "I thought something was going on." She swallowed hard. "What do you need to know?"

## CHAPTER NINETEEN

"Do you know where Hellena is?" Finn asked.

Stephanie shook her head. "Last I knew she said she was traveling out of the country, but that was almost a month ago."

"Traveling for what?" Mila leaned forward, whispering.

"Work, I would guess. She's always on some trip, especially lately."

Finn reached into his pocket to grab his box of Charleston Chews then remembered that Penny had eaten them all. He took a sip of black coffee. "What did she tell you she did?"

Stephanie smirked, angrily wiping at her eyes, her emotions beginning to overflow. "She says she works for a government agency. The CIA or some other acronym. But I knew that was a lie from the beginning. She was always gone, but when she was in town, she didn't go out or talk to people, always acting strange and avoiding public places. Her phone never rang at odd hours like you would expect an agent's phone to do. I realized, pretty early on, that she had to work for herself, or at least not for the government."

Finn leaned back, trying to figure out how to broach the subject of what was going on with this girl's mother, but Mila was miles ahead of him.

Reaching across the table, Mila took Stephanie's hand in hers. The young woman resisted at first, but she quickly giving over to the familiar touch. "I can tell you she doesn't work for the government. The opposite, in fact."

Stephanie choked back a small sob, wiping at her eyes with her free hand. "I was afraid of that. She's been changing lately, becoming angry at the drop of a hat, and traveling more than usual. When she did come home, she was different. She seemed like someone else the last time I saw her. It was like she was only there because she had to be. We talked once in the three days she was home, and she was saying weird things the whole time."

"Like what?" Finn asked, shifting to give Penny a little more room in his jacket.

"She said that the world was about to change for the better, but that it was going to be a hard time for those who didn't know their own power," Stephanie said, staring into her latte.

Mila squeezed her hand and gave her a small smile. "Was that the last time you talked to her?"

Stephanie shook her head. "She called me a week ago." She swallowed, working up the courage to continue. "She said that people were going to start talking about her, and not to believe them. But that didn't make sense if she was some kind of spy or whatever she was pretending to be. I didn't know who to tell. I didn't even know if I should tell anyone. She sent men to watch over me, but they kept me at the house when I wasn't in class. They scared me. It was like I was in prison." She looked up and gave a sad smile. "Today was the first time I didn't see them parked out on the street in a week."

Finn nodded. "Yeah. We had a bit of a run-in with them earlier. They won't be bothering you anymore."

"Good. The bald guy acted like my mother was some kind of religious leader. It was creepy."

"Yeah, he wasn't exactly all there." Mila nodded. "I have to ask, why are you so willing to tell us this? Don't get me wrong, I appreciate it, but you don't know the first thing about us."

Stephanie laughed, making her have to wipe her nose with a napkin. "That's the thing. I do know about you two. She called me last week and warned me that there might be a large man with a beard and a small Mexican woman snooping around and that I should avoid you. She told me that you would tell me lies about her."

Finn cocked his head to the side. "Then why are you talking to us?"

"I don't trust her anymore," Stephanie confessed. "She's changed, and I think she's about to do something terrible. If you're the ones she wants to keep me from, then I need to talk to you. She scares me. I don't know what happened to her, but she's not my mother anymore, at least not the mother I remember. I need help."

Mila squeezed her hand. "We're here to help, Stephanie. We need to stop what Hellena is about to do. I don't know how much I can say or how much you know about what she is, but she has a darkness consuming her from the inside. I don't know if we can stop it without hurting her, but we have to stop what's coming, or a lot of people are going to die."

Stephanie considered Mila's words, sniffing hard. "I don't know where she is, but I have a way to find her. If you help me get out of here and away from her people, I'll help you."

"We can do that," Finn assured her. "We should get out of town soon, though. I have no idea how many people she has under her influence, but I'm sure the guys we ran into earlier aren't the last of them."

Stephanie's breath caught in her throat as she looked past Finn through the front window. "Too late. They're here."

Finn looked and saw two Humvees parking in the small lot. As the vehicles stopped, the doors opened, and four guys in full tactical gear piled out, heading for the front door at a run.

Finn didn't hesitate, sliding out of the booth, pulling Mila out with him, then taking Stephanie's hand and pulling her to her feet. "We need to go." He pointed to the rear exit. "Out the back, quickly." He pushed Stephanie to a run, pulling Mila along with him.

Mila caught on and whispered the power word for her armor as she pulled the Ivar from its holster.

Finn reached past Stephanie and shoved the back door open, herding the young woman out into the alley. They skidded to a stop when twenty rifles were leveled at them held by soldiers in black tactical gear matching that of the men who were coming in from the front door. After a beat, the eight men came out the back door, joining their comrades and pointing rifles at them.

Finn slowly spun around, taking in the threat. They were surrounded, and Finn wasn't sure he could get them out of this one.

A man wearing a red beret stepped forward, not saying a thing, but holding out a phone, the screen showing a connected call. Finn hesitated, but the man motioned for him to take the phone, his face hard.

Finn stepped forward and took it. Holding the phone to his ear, he cleared his throat. "Hello?"

"Do I have your attention, dwarf?" Hellena said, ice in her voice.

"Yeah. You do, Hellena. What can I do for you?" Finn said, taking the phone from his ear and putting the call on speakerphone.

"You can fucking die." She shouted, before continuing in a menacing tone. "How dare you go after my daughter. She is mine. Do you hear me? Mine! You've gone too far, dwarf. No one takes what's mine and lives to talk about it. I am coming for you and your little Valkyrie. I'll make you watch as I peel the skin from her living body and feed it to my dogs. I'll find your little elf friend and your fucking goblin pets and make you watch as I have them drawn and quartered. And when that's all done, I'll drive a knife into your heart as slow as I can to be sure I see the moment you expire. Your precious city will be the first I wipe off the map, a sacrifice to my grand design. It will be the perfect catalyst to start the war and finally take what is mine."

The men became a little uncomfortable as their leader shouted through the little speaker, but were too afraid to say anything. Finn gave them all a knowing look, but that just seemed to anger them even more.

A sniff made Finn look over to see Stephanie in a state of shock at hearing her mother's threats. Tears rolled down her cheeks, and she made no attempt to wipe them away.

The silence drew out, and it began to snow large fat flakes. Several times Stephanie opened her mouth to say something, only to close it again when the words didn't come.

Hellena, growing impatient, growled like an animal. "I've had enough of your trouble. You were the fly that landed in my soup. It's time I dealt with you once and—"

"Mom?" Stephanie said, her voice thick with emotion.

The Dark Star quieted at her daughter's words, understanding that Stephanie had heard her. "You will pay for this, Dwarf King."

"Mom?" Stephanie sniffed again, wiping her nose with the sleeve of her sweater. "Why are you doing this? Finn and Mila haven't done anything to hurt me. It's you who keeps me under guard, locked up in that house like some kind of animal. Why are you doing this?"

Finn could hear Hellena breathing through clenched teeth. "You will understand, one day, Steph."

"I need to understand now," Stephanie demanded, her voice becoming hard. "The things you said; those aren't the things a sane person says, Mom. What's happened to you? How did you get like this?"

"I sought the power to make our lives better. That power comes at a cost. You'll understand one day—"

"That's not good enough," Stephanie shouted. "You talk about peeling the skin from a live person like you've done it before. I don't know who you are anymore. I would rather flee with complete strangers than be forced to see you again. Do you know what that's like? You took the only person I could count on away from me. Somehow I lost you, and I don't know why! Tell me what is happening!"

Hellena's voice went cold and emotionless. "That's enough. No one tells me what I can and can't do. You will be returned home, and I will collect you when I am ready. Anders, kill the dwarf and Valkyrie, and be sure you don't miss the little shit of a dragon."

The line went dead.

Anders raised his gun along with his men. "Fire!"

Finn dropped to his knee, expecting a little more time and began to gather his magic, but he knew it was too late.

Then Stephanie clapped her hands over her head and began to scream.

The sound was piercing. It grew as the seconds drew out. No one fired a shot and, Finn felt the blood in his head throbbing. His vision went white at the edges. Mila dropped to a knee beside him, trying in vain to plug her ears, her eyes screwed shut, and teeth clenched.

Just when Finn thought he was going to lose consciousness, the sound stopped, and something in the air cracked as if a glass shell had shattered into a billion shards. A blast of raw power and the colors of a supernova exploded away from Stephanie.

The soldiers blasted backward as the shockwave reached them, throwing bodies into brick walls, dumpsters, or hurtling them end over end down the alley. Finn heard hundreds of bones snapping as the men were broken against the hard surfaces.

The snow, having been blasted away, began to fall again as Stephanie stumbled and fell backward.

Finn caught her in his arms and surveyed the damage. Bodies littered the alley, and as far as he could tell, none of them would be moving ever again. At least not under their own power. Mila shakily stood, blinking to clear her vision as Penny crawled out of his jacket, her eyes wide as she stared at Stephanie.

"Chi." Penny pointed at the unconscious girl, wonder in her voice.

Finn did as she suggested and took a look at Stephanie's aura. "Holy shitcakes. She's brighter than the sun. Where the hell did that come from?"

"What?" Mila asked, not having learned how to see auras yet.

"You know how I said she didn't have an aura?"

Mila nodded. "Yeah. You said it was locked away."

"Well, it isn't anymore. This girl is bright as a beacon."

The sound of sirens in the distance made them both glance down the alley. "We should probably get out of here," Mila said. "We need to get her someplace safe."

Finn nodded and started jogging down the alley towards Stephanie's house. "I really wish we had driven. Carrying an unconscious girl down the road is pretty suspicious behavior."

"You want me to go get the car while you wait here with all the dead bodies?" Mila suggested.

"Har har." Finn frowned at her. "No. I want us to run."

Mila and Finn ran, Penny on his shoulder and Stephanie in his arms. Mila, keeping pace, asked, "Where to?"

"Home." Finn puffed. "It's the safest place I can think with the wards Penny put up."

"Man, Danica is going to pop her top when I bring another wayward magical home with me."

"Especially when we tell her who she is. Nothing like stealing a madwoman's child to get her to come to you."

"I don't know. Hellena sounded damn cold on the phone. I don't know how much mother is left."

"It's the way dark magic works. It eats the soul of the user till there is nothing left but a power-hungry shell. At least until the body gives out. Dark magic is always a death sentence for the user; it just takes time."

# CHAPTER TWENTY

M ila took Route 36, keeping the Hellcat at a reasonable speed for once. The chase earlier must have gotten a lot of pent up aggressive driving out of her system.

Looking into the backseat, he checked on their passenger for the hundredth time. Stephanie hadn't moved a muscle since he had lain her across the bench seat. Penny perched beside her, gently stroking her head and using her powers to soothe the girl's emotions.

"She okay?" Mila asked.

Finn nodded as he turned back to look out the windshield. "Yeah. Still hasn't moved. She used a lot of power back there. Probably did her a real number."

The snow was coming down, especially between Boulder and Denver. A front of heavy clouds pushed their way south along the Rockies and dumped their contents on the metro area. The visibility was awful.

"About that," Mila said, slowing since the snowfall was

picking up. "What exactly was that spell? It didn't look like peabrain magic or even elf magic. It was wilder."

"Shir shee chi," Penny said from the back.

"A witch?" Mila raised an eyebrow. "Isn't a witch just a female human magic-user?"

Finn chuckled. "Why would you think that? A human magic-user is called a Peabrain."

Mila frowned and gave him a quick side glance to see if he was messing with her. "Isn't a Peabrain what magicals call a nonmagic user?"

Finn nodded. "Yeah. Just because they forgot how to use magic doesn't make them any less a Peabrain."

"Okay, putting that aside for now, what's a witch?"

"They're a race of people, like peabrains or elves or dwarves. They're a people."

"And they have a different kind of magic?" Mila had a confused look on her face, having trouble grasping this.

Finn chewed his tongue as he thought how to explain. "Sort of. Magic is energy. It's everywhere and, pretty much, in everything. Every race has a different way of channeling it. Peabrains, for example, have a tiny spot in the back of their brains that allows them to tap into magical energy, so that little spot, or 'peabrain' if you will, is like a bridge from their bodies to the magical power. They only use what they need, letting it flow through them. Does that make sense?"

Mila nodded, her scientific brain digesting the information. "So, how are the other races different?"

"Well, dwarves don't have a peabrian, so we have to channel our power differently. We use earth, drawing the power into us as we walk around touching the ground. We have to store that power inside, so we can use all our power up and be left with nothing, like when I used that large area of effect spell when we were going after the hellhounds."

"Oh, yeah. Hermin had to bring you some rocks that Penny shoved down your throat."

"I pulled the magic out of them, but I have to be careful doing it that way, I could have taken in too much and killed myself," Finn said, holding up a hand to stop the comment he saw coming. "Penny knows what I can take. She wouldn't have given me too much."

"Chi," Penny said, making Finn blanch.

"What? You were guessing?" He glared over his shoulder.

Penny shrugged. "Shir?"

"You're sorry?" Finn was stunned.

"Chi shir shee," the dragon said, with an indignant toss of her head.

Finn frowned, turning back, and crossing his arms. "Yeah. It worked. I can't believe you were guessing."

Mila glanced to see if he was done pouting before continuing, "So, how do witches use magic? Actually, how do I use magic?" Her eyebrows rose as she realized just how little she knew.

Finn blew out a long breath. "Well, witches are a bit of a mix between dwarves and peabrains. Like dwarves, they collect magic and store it, but they can get it from everything around them, unlike dwarves who need rock or dirt. Then they have to use a wand to focus the power like peabrains do through that small spot in their brain. As for you? I honestly have no idea. There's one big difference between you and the rest of us. You don't use the same magical energy we do. You use celestial magic, and I have to be honest; I don't know the first thing about it, except that it's not the same energy I use."

Mila frowned.

Finn saw the expression and patted her knee. "Sorry, darlin'. You're just going to have to accept you're a special snowflake."

Her shoulders shook with a silent chuckle. "You're such a dork."

"Squee!" Penny shouted, making Finn spin around.

Stephanie was starting to rouse. Her eyes fluttered, and she groaned in pain, her arms and legs drawing her into the fetal position. Penny put a hand on her forehead and began to channel some of her healing power to ease the girl's mind.

Stephanie's eyes snapped open. She stared at Penny for a second, only inches away from her face, before screaming and scrambling across the backseat, her knees in her chest and hands out towards Penny. There was a deep concussive blast, and Penny was thrown off the bench seat and onto the floor as the rear end of the car slammed into the road, making the shocks bounce the wheels off the pavement then slamming down again.

Mila had to think fast to keep them from spinning out from the jolt.

"Penny! You okay?" Finn shouted, reaching around and scooping her up in one hand.

"Chi," she groaned, shaking her head.

"Where am I?" Stephanie shouted, her eyes manic, as another spell went off.

This time Finn's seat was slammed forward, and he was pressed into his seatbelt hard enough to leave a bruise.

"Stephanie, you're safe! Calm down!" Mila shouted, swerving into her lane as the car was rocked by another blast.

"What's happening? Why are things exploding?" the young woman was frantic, her feet scrambling, trying to get her away from what was happening to her, but she was already pressed against the door.

She flicked her fingers as if trying to get something off of them, and a wave of raw power sliced out from her fingers, leaving a clean cut in the leather upholstery that went all the way to the ceiling. The glass of the back window had a new hair-thin slice through it that whistled as air passed over it.

"We need to get her out of the car. She's going to rip this thing apart from the inside," Finn said, keeping his voice low to not alarm the panicking girl.

Mila glanced at the long slice in her precious car, a pained expression crossing her face before she nodded, stepping on the gas.

Luckily they were coming to the end of the long stretch of 36, and the McCaslin Boulevard exit was in less than a quarter-mile.

Finn tried to calm Stephanie, even suggesting Penny try to soothe her again, but the sight of the tiny dragon had Stephanie freaking out and rocking the car with another energy blast. This time, the back window spider-webbed with cracks, and one of the back seat cushions exploded, sending foam and leather scraps all over the interior of the car.

Mila groaned and took the exit at speed. She turned right at the light, barely slowing and making the tires squeal as she drifted slightly. She spotted a Phillips 66 on the right and slammed on the brakes. Spinning the wheel and hopping a bit of curb, she raced between the main building and the car wash, Mila jammed on the brakes and slid the Hellcat into a parking space at the back of the station.

Finn was out of the car in a flash, shoving the front seat forward, and reaching into the back to grab hold of Stephanie's hand. He pulled her out of the car, trying not to hurt the girl. She stumbled and fell into him, sending a shock through him that threw him onto his ass and stunned him somewhat.

His head swam as the electric shock dissipated, sending sparks between his fingers. He watched, unable to move or say anything, as Mila came racing around the car, and threw her arms around the shellshocked Stephanie.

Both women froze in place.

Finn struggled to get to his feet, his jaw clenched from the shock, and his muscles not working correctly. Penny came bounding out of the car, a healing potion in one hand she had pulled from the glove box; they had learned the hard way to always keep a few extras in the car. She slid to a stop at his side and uncorked the vial, before flapping her wings and lifting the tube of red liquid to his lips. It was all Finn could do to open his mouth even a tiny bit, but he managed, and Penny dumped the contents into his mouth.

Nearly ten seconds later, Finn was able to swallow the potion. His muscles began to knit together, the extreme shock having ripped them as they strained to all flex at once. After another thirty seconds, he was able to move again if a little stiffly.

Finn climbed to his feet and stumbled a little as he stepped close to the two women. At first, he thought they were locked in some kind of continual electric shock and feared the worst, but when he got close, Finn realized they were just standing there, not moving at all. He reached out a tentative hand and touched Mila's shoulder. Both women rocked on their feet as Finn put some pressure into the touch. As far as he could see, they were fine, just not moving.

"Thanks," Finn said to Penny as she landed on his shoulder and accepted a fist bump. "I didn't realize how bad that was. I can't believe the power she has."

"Shir."

Finn frowned, not knowing what to do. He didn't know if the two women were locked in place because of Stephanie's power or Mila's. When he tried to view their auras, both of them were blazing like bonfires, their magic swirling together, but not seeming to be doing anything.

"What the fuck is going on?"

Penny shrugged. "Squee shir?"

Finn's eyebrow rose. "Not a bad idea. She might have seen something like this before. Worth a shot, I guess."

He pulled out his phone and found Danica's number, but before he could hit the call button, an employee from the gas station came around the corner, a pack of cigarettes in his hand.

"Oh, hey, man." The pimpled youth said, shocked to find anyone in his smoking spot.

He glanced over at Mila with her arms wrapped around

Stephanie's ribcage and her face buried in the taller woman's chest. Stephanie had her arms up as if surrendering to the cops. It was a weird tableau.

"Uh, what the fuck?" the young man said, a cigarette halfway out of the pack.

"They're practicing to be living statues," Finn said, remembering when Mila had explained the performance art when they saw a man painted chrome standing on the side of the street one night.

The kid nodded, then put the cigarette in his mouth and lit it. "They're good," he said, smoke billowing out of his mouth. "Is that a dragon?" he pointed to Penny, who was stock-still on Finn's shoulder.

Finn looked over at the same time as Penny. They stared at one another for a second. "Yup. Sure is."

"Cool." The kid said, pulling out his phone, opening some social media app, and slowly scrolling through it.

Finn watched the kid for a full minute, but he seemed disinterested in what was happening beyond his screen.

Finn shrugged and called Danica.

# CHAPTER TWENTY-ONE

Mila opened her eyes, expecting to be in a hospital after seeing what Stephanie had done to Finn, but there was a driving need Mila had felt deep in her core to help this poor girl whose world had been turned inside out.

To Mila's great surprise, she did not find herself in a hospital. In fact, she didn't find herself anywhere. She blinked a few times in the hope that she was just dazed or something, but all she could see was complete and utter darkness. She still felt Stephanie in her arms, but she couldn't see her at all even though her face was pressed against the girl's sweater.

Panic set in. Mila wished there was light. She blinked and, when her eyes opened again, the blackness had been replaced with a sourceless white light that emanated from everywhere. Mila pulled back and saw Stephanie, her eyes still wide with terror and confusion, her arms held above her head, but she was unmoving. Even her long red curls were held aloft in defiance of gravity.

"Stephanie?" Mila said quietly. She stepped forward and pressed two fingers to the girl's neck, feeling for a pulse but found nothing. Her skin was still warm and supple under Mila's fingers, but there was no bodily response she could find.

"Stephanie?" she said a little louder, shaking her by the shoulders.

Nothing.

Mila spun, looking for anything that might help her figure out where the hell she was, but the endless white light extended forever in all directions.

"Shit. I'm in the fucking Matrix."

"That's a pretty apt description," a deep female voice said from behind Mila.

Spinning, Mila reached the holster on the back of her corset, pulling the Ivar out and pointing it at a tall, pretty woman with long wavy blonde hair. The woman wore a black pinstripe suit that had obviously been tailored to fit her perfectly. She stood with her arms crossed and a stern look on her face as she appraised Mila. In all ways, she looked like a normal Caucasian woman...except for wings of pure light coming out of her back.

Mila's eyes widened. She turned her head from side to side to see them from tip to tip. They glowed a warm golden color and seemed to be translucent, but it was hard to tell with the white background. There were no feathers; instead, the wings were made up of sharp lines and angles that hinted more at the idea of wings rather than functional appendages.

As Mila watched, the thirty-foot wingspan faded, becoming thinner and thinner until only a wisp of golden light remained, which twisted and twirled away as if on a light breeze. Eventually, even that faded to nothing.

"That won't work here, but I do have to admire your reaction time." The woman said with a slight smile. "Quite impressive."

"Who are you?" Mila asked, not putting the pistol away, but lowering it a few inches.

"I was about to ask you the same thing." The tall woman said, dropping her arms and strolling around Mila and Stephanie at a leisurely pace, her stiletto heels making a tapping noise with each step as if the ground were made of marble. "I thought you were Genevive at first, being so short with that dark hair, but you're the new one, aren't you?" a smile lit her lips.

"New what?" Mila asked, wearily. She didn't turn her body, but she did track the woman with her eyes.

She laughed, tossing her blonde hair over her shoulder. "The new sister. You're a Valkyrie, are you not?"

Mila's eyes widened. "You're a Valkyrie? Like me?"

The woman stopped walking, having made a full circuit and ending where she had begun. She spread her hands out to encompass the endless void. "Of course. How else could we be here together?"

Mila looked around. "I don't know where this is, let alone the rules here."

"This is Elsewhere. The place between life and death."

"I'm dead?"

The woman looked at her with concern. "Do you not have any memories of this place?"

"Why would I? I've never been here before," Mila said with exasperation.

This seemed to bother the woman. "That isn't possible. You should have the memories of your past lives. Of the sisters that contained you through the millennia. When I spoke to your friend Gregory, I thought it was odd you hadn't contacted us directly, but I had no idea you didn't know how."

Mila set her jaw. She was just about done with this conversation. "Look, lady. I don't know how this usually happens, but I didn't even know magic existed until a few months ago, let alone I was a Valkyrie. If I'm supposed to have some head full of memories, I must have missed the download. It's just me in here." She said, tapping her temple with a finger. "If you would be so kind, please explain what the fuck is going on. How did I get here, and how do I get back?"

The woman cleared her throat. "I'm sorry. This is very unusual. My name is Victoria. I'm the head sister at the moment. Please forgive my flippant comments. You have to understand there are only so many Valkyries on Earth. I assumed you were one of the sisters that had not returned after her last death. There is always a handful of us missing while we wait for new bodies to be selected. If you truly have no memories of past lives, then you must be a First-born. We didn't think it was possible anymore."

Mila sighed and, reaching around her back, put the Ivar in its holster. She extended a hand to Victoria. "I'm Mila. And I promise you, I have only my own memories. I don't really know what that means, but I'm sure we can have a nice long conversation about it in the future. Right now, I really need to get back home, and I have a feeling that I need to help Stephanie here before I go. Can you help me?"

Victoria shook Mila's offered hand then looked the red-headed woman over, compassion at Stephanie's palpable terror coming through in her eyes. "I can not help with this, but you can do it yourself. I assume Gregory conveyed my message to you?"

"Yeah, something about how my power comes from my conviction, not my desire?"

"Correct." Victoria smiled kindly. "It is not enough to want a thing, you will need to believe it is also for the best for your powers to work. If you truly are a Firstborn, it will take time for your powers to fully manifest, but helping this poor soul is well within your reach." She considered something before continuing, "Unless you want to change her powers. You could do it, but I must warn you the cost is steep, and we would need to bring the Reaper."

Mila raised a questioning eyebrow. "The Grim Reaper?"

Victoria laughed, her rich voice making it a pleasure to hear. "No, dear. The artifact. The Reaper." Victoria shook her head. "Right. It's going to take some getting used to having a new Valkyrie among us."

Mila wanted to roll her eyes at being called a Firstborn, but she refrained. From the other Valkyrie's perspective, she guessed she was rather like a newborn.

"The Reaper is why we are here in the first place. It is the secret we all must keep, but it defines us as a sister-hood." She pursed her lips. "I'm guessing that you do not want to change her powers since you didn't know it was a possibility. That is good. Reaping is far too costly for one like you—a topic for a later time."

"If I believe helping Stephanie is for the greater good, then what?"

"Then do it. It's really that simple. But you must truly believe it will help. Otherwise, nothing will happen. Our powers cannot be used for frivolous things, a blessing in disguise over a long enough life. You will see." Victoria smiled, putting her hands on her hips. "I have a feeling there is something special about you—a greater role to play than you know."

Mila didn't know how to take that last part. "Thanks, I think." She looked back at Stephanie. "So, how do I take us home after I'm done?"

"Simply will it to happen." Victoria spread her hands out. "We hold dominion over this place. Our will is enough to make things reality here."

Mila turned to Stephanie. "Okay. I guess I'll give it a try."

There was no reply, and when Mila looked for Victoria, the Valkyrie was nowhere to be seen. She turned back to Stephanie. She felt compassion for Hellena's daughter in a way that went to Mila's core. Hellena had imprisoned her own daughter, kept her magic sealed away, then Stephanie finds out the only family she has left wants to start a war. To top it off, oh yeah, magic is a real thing, and she can't stop setting off destructive spells every two damn seconds.

Mila thought about what she would have wanted to know the day she found out magic was real. The small details that kept the magical world running and how she could fit into it. She gathered her memories of all the conversations she and Finn and Penny had had over their time together. She thought about Danica and her unique form of healing magic. She included the conversation about how witches needed wands to focus their power, not that she had a lot of knowledge on the subject.

She took all those thoughts and brought them together. Once she understood how it would make Stephanie's life better, she coalesced those understandings into a conviction—Stephanie *needed* to know.

There was a feeling of everything clicking into place in the back of Mila's mind, and she knew it would all work out. She wrapped her arms around Stephanie and felt the power flow from her into the young woman.

# CHAPTER TWENTY-TWO

F inn glanced over at the pimply kid, as the phone rang, but he was still engrossed in his memes and cigarette.

The call connected, and Finn turned to focus on Mila and Stephanie.

"Hello, my friend!" Danica answered, sounding ready to take on the day, even though the sun was starting to set.

"Danica. We have a bit of a problem. Penny thought you might be able to help," Finn said, his tone somber.

"I'll do my best. By the way, I got you a little surprise from the mall. Mila will love it," she said mischievously.

"I can't wait. First, though, we might need to wake Mila up."

There was a pause. "I don't get it," Danica confessed.

Finn related the story of how Mila grabbed onto Stephanie, and they both froze. He told the tail quickly, leaving out the more extensive details, like who Stephanie was and the fact that Penny had been passing out in the twisted magic, but Dani got the gist.

"Are they breathing?" the elf asked in her medical voice, all playfulness gone.

Finn double-checked, looking to see that both of their chests were rising and falling at a slow and steady pace. "It appears they are. I would say it's a little slow considering the circumstances."

"Okay, take their pulses. I need an estimate."

"Hang on." He handed the phone to Penny, who was watching from his shoulder, then reached out with both hands, placing two fingers lightly on both women's necks and began to count. After ten seconds or so, he took the phone back. "Mila's is around sixty and Stephanie's is closer to eighty."

"That's good. Can you move them? Or are they rigid, like their muscles are locked up?" Danica's calmness kept Finn's anxiety under control.

Finn gently tried to lower one of Stephanie's arms. He expected her to stay in the same position, but her arm lowered. When he let go, it stayed where he had positioned it.

"I can move them."

"Interesting. Can you drive the Hellcat?"

The question caught him so off guard he had to do a restart, opening his mouth, then closing it as the problem registered, and he glanced over at the large black muscle car. "I've driven it before; the first time I met Mila, actually," he said fondly, remembering their first interaction at the Kum & Go.

"She let you drive her car? She doesn't let anyone drive her car."

"She lets you drive it all the time when we use the Subaru."

"That's different. Mila lets me do anything. I'm her best friend."

"I'm her man-friend, and she doesn't let me drive it."

"That's different. And, for the love of all that is holy, don't use the word man-friend! It's so not right. Here's what I want you to do. Get them both in the car and bring them straight here. It sounds like whatever is going on isn't an immediate threat, but I need to see them to better figure this out."

Finn nodded, stepping up to the two snow-covered women. He hesitated. "What if separating them does something? Like, there's a connection I break, and they get stuck this way."

"Shee shir?"

"Never mind, Danica. Penny figured it out. Okay, we're about twenty minutes away. Meet me out front of the condo. I don't want some stranger to think I'm kidnapping two women."

"How will my being there stop someone from doing that?"

"Because you're a pretty woman, and people don't associate pretty women as creeps. A six-five bearded guy, however?"

Danica was silent for a few seconds. "I hate to admit it, but that makes sense. Okay, I'll meet you out front in twenty."

Finn hung up and dropped his phone in his jacket pocket while he tried to figure out the best way to lift them both without hurting them.

"Can you open it up while I get these two?" Finn asked Penny, who gave him a nod and launched herself towards the open passenger door.

Finn stepped up beside the two women and squatted so that his chest was even with Mila's but sideways relative to her body. He wrapped his arms around them, pulling both in so their sides were against his chest. He stood and lifted them a good two feet off the ground, then he slowly walked to the back of the car as Penny popped the trunk.

"Can you fold the backseats down?" he called to Penny as he slowly tilted the women to the side so that Mila was now mostly laying on Stephanie.

The left side of the split backseat went down, followed by the right. Now there was a good six or seven feet of flat surface to lay them on, but holding them by the waist like he was, he was not able to simultaneously lay them inside the trunk and get out of the way of the trunk's edge.

"Dude. Those girls are dedicated as fuck to this living statue thing."

Finn snapped his head around and saw the kid standing behind him, watching him struggle with the awkward load.

"Uh, yeah. They really like to use the method acting process." Finn hesitated a second. "I don't suppose you would help me get them in the trunk?"

The kid shrugged. "Sure. I still have five minutes."

Finn had the kid take their feet while he did the heavy work of gently feeding their heads and torsos into the now-folded down backseat. After a minute or two, the girls were half in the trunk and half in the backseat, still entwined in each other's arms. Finn took a minute to reposition them into the most comfortable position he could manage, then closed the trunk.

"Thanks. I'm glad you were here to help," Finn said, shaking the kid's hand.

"No problem, man. That's why I'm in the service industry," he said flatly.

"Good for you. It's nice to know what you want to do with the rest of your life at such a young age."

The kid smirked. "Dude, it was a joke. I work here because my dad made me get a job."

Finn slapped him on the shoulder. "Still. It might grow on you. Who's to say."

"Whatever, man. Take her easy." He sauntered off around the building towards the front.

"What a helpful young man," Finn said to Penny as he climbed into the driver's seat and cracked his knuckles.

Penny rolled her eyes. "Shir?"

"Yeah, I'm serious. I like to think that kid's got a bright future ahead. Out here helping people in need." Finn pressed the start button, and the Hellcat roared to life.

Penny cocked her head at him, a look of disbelief plastered across her face. "Squee shir chi!"

Finn waved the comment away. "He didn't help me kidnap two women off the street. They're my friends."

"Chi."

Finn thought about that as he pulled the car out of the parking space and drove around the building towards the main road.

"I suppose you're right. He didn't actually know they were my friends." Finn looked through the large glass window at the kid, now behind the counter, his face once again buried in his phone. "What a creepy little dude."

---

Seventeen minutes later, Finn pulled into an empty space at the front of their condo building. Ever since they bought out the rest of the tenants' units, parking around the building had become much more accessible.

True to her word, Danica was standing in the small lobby, watching for them through the glass door and windows, and came out to meet them before Finn was even out of the car. He popped the trunk and closed the driver's door as Danica looked in the backseat and saw the top halves of the two women.

"Seriously? Penny's great idea was to put them in the trunk like bags of groceries?" Danica said with a disappointed look.

"It worked, didn't it?" Finn argued, going around to the back of the car and reaching in to grab both Mila and Stephanie by a thigh. "Get inside and help with their shoulders."

Danica sighed and climbed into the back of the Challenger, helping to maneuver her friend and their new charge out of the awkward space.

Two minutes—and lots of cursing—later, Finn was able to carry them into the building while Danica held the door. They received a few odd looks, but more out of curiosity than anything. It wasn't every day you saw someone pulling two rigid people from a trunk and take them into a condo building in downtown Denver.

Finn stood the two women up in the elevator, and Danica hit the button for the fourth floor. She began checking on the two immediately, taking their pulse and feeling for fever or chill with the back of her hand.

On the ride up, Finn heard the distinct sound of hammering and sawing on the second floor. "Did they already start construction?"

Danica nodded, using a stethoscope she pulled from around her neck to listen to first Mila then Stephanie's heart. "Yeah, Kevin and his guy showed up around noon raring to get started. I called Remmy like you asked. She had a few suggestions, but nothing too extravagant. Kevin wanted to get a jumpstart on the project, so I gave him a key to the building, and he brought his crew back this afternoon. Me and Remmy have been playing Mario Kart ever since."

"Is she any good?"

"Better than me, but she wouldn't hold a candle to Penny."

Penny puffed up like a rooster on Finn's shoulder. "Shir, shir."

"I still think you cheat," Danica said, draping her stethoscope over her neck. "No one gets that many blue shells and still wins. I'm pretty sure the game is designed so that can't happen."

Penny gave her the finger, and Danica laughed. "Right back at you, punk."

The elevator opened, and Finn squatted, picking the two up and taking them to the front door. He had to squat-walk to get them through without hitting Stephanie's head on the door frame, but he was soon depositing them on the couch, laying them down along the long part of the L-shaped sectional.

Remmy was on the couch, a small Switch controller in her hand, watching Finn muscle the two ladies inside. "Heya, Boss. Did you steal that girl?"

Finn chuckled. "No, Remmy. I didn't steal her. She needed our help, and we helped."

"Kinda looks like Mila's still helping," Remmy said, crossing her short legs under her. "Either that or she found a replacement for you."

Penny laughed and headed for the kitchen pantry.

"She's not a replacement. We don't know what's happening. Mila grabbed onto her and they just froze up. Penny guessed that they might be in some kind of mind-meld or something. Stephanie had just used her magic for the first time and was kinda freaking out, then Mila stepped in, and they've been like this ever since. Hey! Don't do that!" He admonished Remmy, who had realized very quickly that the two women would stay in the position you put them and bent Stephanie's fingers around until they were both giving the middle finger to the ceiling.

"Sorry, Boss. Gotta get your fun in while you can," she said with a shrug.

"Wise words."

"You betcha. Clan motto. I even have it in one of my tattoos." She pulled down the waist of her jeans, and sure enough, it was written in runes on her hip.

"That explains so much about you," Danica said, her arms crossed as she just shook her head in bewilderment.

"So, what do we do with these two? Are they going to be alright?" Finn asked Danica, who gave a shrug.

"I mean, their vitals are all good as far as I can tell. Nothing seems to be interfering with their systems, they're just not moving. They still have pupil response, but no other kinds of reactions. I think we just have to wait it out."

"This isn't good." Finn sighed, leaning his hands on the back of the couch as he watched Mila's back rise and fall in deep, even breaths. "I need them to wake up. Stephanie has a way to contact her mother, who very recently just told me she wants to murder us all in exciting ways."

"Whoa. Who's her mother?" Danica asked.

Finn fixed Danica with a long stare.

"Oh." The elf got it. "The Dark Star."

Remmy and Danica both gawped at Finn.

"The Dark Star has a kid?"

"Why would you steal the Dark Stars daughter? Didn't we have enough to worry about without you kicking the hornet's nest?"

"I kinda feel like you're collecting women at this point, Boss."

Finn gave Remmy a disapproving stare for that last one.

"It doesn't matter she's pissed at me, and you, by extension," Finn argued. "She was going to carry out her crazy play to establish a country without my interference. Hell, if anything, I'm pushing her in before she's ready."

Danica opened her mouth to argue, but a gasp from Mila sent Danica to her side in an instant. A second later, Stephanie sucked in a deep breath that turned to panicked panting. Before anyone could try to calm her, she saw Mila lying on top of her and cried out with joy, pulling the dazed Valkyrie into a bear hug.

"Oh, thank you. Thank you, thank you." She sobbed into Mila's shoulder.

Mila recovered, wrapping her arms around Stephanie and squeezing her tight. "Trust me, you deserve so much more."

"What the hell is happening?" Finn asked no one in particular.

"I think you've been replaced, Boss. Sorry." Remmy shrugged.

"I need a beer." Finn headed for the kitchen, his head slowly shaking from side to side.

## CHAPTER TWENTY-THREE

Finn opened the fridge and grabbed a beer, twisting the top off and taking a long pull from the bottle.

His pocket vibrated. He pulled his phone out, accidentally hitting the accept button in the process.

"Fuck." He quickly put the phone to his ear. "Hello?"

"I never wanted it to go this way, Finnegan," Hellena said in a calm voice. "I had a plan that would have cost some lives, yes, but it would have been quick and efficient, keeping deaths to a minimum. Then, you fell out of the sky and began rooting around in my plans like a pig snorting out truffles."

"Hello, Hellena. Good to hear from you, too," he said with a sigh as he fell back to lean his ass on the counter. The sound of the girls talking behind him made him keep his voice down. He didn't want to worry them too much if she was just calling to make idle threats again.

"You think you're so funny, don't you, Dwarf King?" Hellena sneered. "Maybe this is all my fault. I wasn't clear enough right from the beginning. It's like they say, 'when you are training a dog, you first have to break its will.'"

Finn screwed up his face in disgust. "Fucking hell, woman. Who taught you how to train a dog? See, this is why people don't like you."

"Your words don't matter anymore. You don't matter anymore. You stole the only thing holding me back. I was going to let Stephanie have her years at college, like a normal girl. My plans would wait until she was gone, protected from the coming war. But you rooted until you found her, then you twisted her to your will, and turned her against me. So be it. What is one more death when I have people to save."

"That's not how this went down at all, Hellena," Finn said, boggled at how she twisted everything. "I didn't *steal* her away. You pushed her away. You're supposed to be her mother, but she's terrified of what you've become. She begged me to take her away from you. I'm not the monster of this story."

Hellena chuckled. "Oh, we are all monsters in someone's story, Finnegan. You just haven't been asking the right people. We're not so different; we both are willing to kill to win. I just have higher aspirations than you. You may not think of yourself as a monster, but when the dust settles and my new nation is formed, who do you think will write the history books? Trust me. You will be seen as you truly are. A brute too stupid to know when to let well enough alone."

Finn had heard plenty of big baddies talking like this over the years. Most of them were nothing more than dust in the wind at this point.

A sigh escaped his lips. "Do you want to know a secret? You want to know why I always win, no matter how many times I get beat down, slapped away, or how uneven the odds are?"

"Please. Enlighten me, Dwarf."

"It's because I don't quit. People like you never seem to learn there's such a thing as a critter that might just keep comin'. So, I'll find you in the end, I promise you that. Just as sure as the turning of the earth."

There was silence on the line for a few beats, then Hellena started laughing. "A John Wayne quote? That's your secret? You can live in your little fantasy world all you want, but out here, the world is going to move on without you. Terrible things are coming, Finnegan. And I want you to know that it's all your fault. I warned you that I would find a way to use the Gjallarhorn. Now hear my triumph."

Finn's jaw dropped open in shock, but the line went dead before he could respond. He spun around in time to see Penny's eyes roll up and she fell limply from the back of the couch and hit the floor.

Danica was in the middle of healing up a few scrapes on Mila's leg from their fight on the mountain, when the warm blue light emanating from her hand turned to a torrent of water, soaking Mila and the couch, making her scream in shock. Danica abolished the spell, shaking her hand as if it had been stung.

A deep rumbling tone began to vibrate the windows. After a second, the noise started to steadily rise in pitch, making everyone clap their hands to their ears. In a matter of moments, the terrible noise culminated in a blast that set their ears ringing, followed by a ripping sound as if the fabric of reality was tearing apart. Glass shattered in three of the window frames, and books fell from the shelves as they vibrated over the edge.

The note cut off abruptly. Besides the ringing in his ears, Finn heard dozens of car alarms on the streets below.

Finn hurdled the kitchen island and slid to his knees beside Penny. He scooped her up and pressed her body to his ear to listen for her heartbeat.

"What the hell is going on?" Stephanie asked, coming around to the back of the couch, along with everyone else.

"Your mother is going on," Mila said heatedly, kneeling beside Finn. "Is she alive?"

Finn nodded. "Just barely. The effects are way worse this time. I'm pretty sure I know what Hellena's machine is doing, and why. She's using it to twist magic so much that the Gjallarhorn recognizes her as dwarven royalty. That's what that sound was. She just used it on something."

"That was my mom?" Stephanie said in shock.

"Yeah, and she's going to keep using it until she starts a war with the Peabrains," Finn said.

"How do we stop it?" Danica asked, her prosthetic hand gripping her other arm in a worried pose.

"Leave that to Mila and me. I need you to get Penny out of the city. She can't take this. That machine is making her magic work against her. If she stays here, she will die. Do you still have the key to Preston's cabin?"

Danica nodded. "Yeah, it's in my room."

"Good, take her there. It should be far enough away that even if the machine affects her, it will be diminished enough, it won't kill her." Finn was cut off when Penny stirred in his hands.

He held her up, so she was close to his face. Her eyes opened, and she blinked slowly, obviously out of it. Finn handed Penny over to Danica.

"Take good care of her. It looks like the machine has been turned off for now, but Hellena could turn it back on any moment. You need to get out of here."

Danica nodded and ran to her room to fetch the key.

A bubble appeared in the middle of the dojo, and when it popped, Hermin and Garret stood there, looking around with angry faces. Spotting everyone, they hurried over.

"That crazy bitch just blew up Preston's estate!" Hermin screamed with rage.

"Somehow, she used the Gjallarhorn," Garret added.

"I know. That's why magic has been twisting on and off. She has a machine or artifact that is making the horn think she's a royal dwarf. She and her people must have been testing it for the last few days."

"You need to stop her. With that machine running, we don't have any way to take her out. We can still operate on the outskirts of its influence, but if she's close to it, we would be useless," Hermin said, his anger softening to horror.

"Don't worry," Finn assured him. "Mila and I are unaffected by the machine. It doesn't work on me because it's attuning magic to what I already am, and Mila uses celestial magic, so she draws her power from another source. Penny, on the other hand, is in a bad way. Hermin, I need you to teleport Danica and Penny to Preston's cabin. Penny can't survive that machine."

Just then, Danica came out of her room, a sling made

from a thin, green patterned scarf tied around her neck and torso, cradling Penny's barely moving form.

"Danica, Hermin will take you to the cabin. You guys need to leave right now before she turns that damned thing on again. Garret, we're going to need some kind of distraction to keep the Peabrains off the streets. The last thing we want is to defeat the Dark Star but still have a war because too many people saw too much."

Garret nodded. "We're way ahead of you on that front. Right now, the boys are down there, cranking up the snow production. We should have a pretty good blizzard blowing in about ten minutes."

"Be careful, guys. I love you." Danica shouted from the dojo, where Hermin was preparing to teleport. She waved with one hand while keeping Penny steady with the other.

"I love you, too. Take care of Penny. We'll see you when this is all over," Mila shouted.

"Look after her, and don't let her try and run off to join us. Trust me, she will try," Finn warned with a wave.

Hermin formed a giant bubble, and they stepped into it. There was a small *pop,* and they were gone.

"What do I do?" Stephanie asked, an overwhelmed look on her face, yet she was still stepping up.

Finn smiled. "I knew I was going to like you. You, my dear, have the most important job of all."

Her eyes went wide, and she brushed a thick lock of red curls from her face. "I do?"

Nodding, Finn put a hand on her shoulder. "You said if we helped you escape, you would tell us how to find your mother. It's time to fulfill that promise. How do we find her?"

Stephanie swallowed and reached into the pocket of her jeans, pulling out what looked like a distress clicker an older person would wear in case of a fall. It was white and relatively thin and had one small button in the center of one flat side.

"She said if I was ever in real danger, I should press the button three times, and I would be taken to her immediately. She made me carry it all the time, even punishing me if she found out I left it at home. I asked her how it worked, but she wouldn't tell me, just saying that it would only work one time, and to be sure it was the last option."

Finn held out his hand. "Sounds like a teleporter to me. That is exactly what I hoped for. Can I have it?"

Stephanie gave him a pained, tight-lipped smile and shook her head. "I can't."

Finn's eyebrow rose suspiciously. "But that was our deal."

"You don't understand, I can't give it to you because it won't work for you. Mom made it very clear it would only work for me. I have to go with you." She was shaking with fear, but her voice was steady.

Finn stared at Stephanie for several long seconds before turning away and staring out the window at the thickening snowfall.

"Fuck!" he shouted, his frustration getting the better of him.

A small hand tapped him on the hip, and he looked down to see Remmy smiling at him with her sharp teeth. "Hey, Boss. We want to help too." She held up one of the in-ear comm devices they had used up at the lake. "You find the fight, and my tribe will meet you there. You'll need lots of back-ups, I'm thinking. We goblins are good fight-ers, and we owe you one."

Finn was shocked. He reached down and took the earpiece. "Remmy, you don't owe me anything. This isn't your fight; there's no need for you and your people to get hurt over this."

Remmy scoffed. "Are you joking, Boss? How is this not our fight? If you lose, then the whole city gets blown away by some dumb horn. Fuck that. Goblins fight!"

Finn accepted the offer. "You're right. I'm sorry, Remmy, it's not my place to tell you what you can and can't fight for. You better hurry, though. I have a feeling this is all going to go down soon."

Remmy gave him an evil grin. "Just tell us where to be, and we'll be there with knives out." She turned and ran to the door, throwing it open and dashing into the hall.

"Did she seem a little eager to you?" Mila asked, concerned.

"Finn, there's something else you need to know," Garret said, wringing his hands. "The Earth is not happy with how much corruption the Dark Star has been spreading. Whole sections of forest have been found flattened or burned, most likely tests with the Gjallarhorn. She's taken notice and dispatched the Dirt Elemental to clean up the mess."

Finn cocked an eyebrow. "The Dirt Elemental?"

"Yeah. He's a bit of an avatar, and a bit of a sentient being. He's the hands of Earth, going around fixing big problems that are getting, well, out of hand. We don't see him much, but when we do, it means trouble. He's not all that fast of a traveler, but you just need to be aware he might show up."

"What does he look like?" Mila asked, fascinated.

Garret shrugged. "Like a giant man of dirt and roots. What else would someone called the Dirt Elemental look like?"

"Good point."

Finn crossed his arms. "If he does show up, is he going to fight with us or try and take us all down?"

"Oh, he will fight alongside you," Garret assured him. "Earth has her eye on you. We're pretty sure she likes you."

"Pretty sure?"

Garret waggled a hand. "Reasonably sure."

CHAPTER TWENTY-FOUR

"Okay," Finn put a comforting hand on Stephanie's shoulder, "you're going to have to come with us, Stephanie. We'll do our best to protect you, but I'm not going to lie, this is going to be rough. When we get there, I'm going to need you to find a good hiding spot right away. Can you do that?"

She nodded, her thick red curls bobbing up and down at the ends. "Press the button, find a hiding spot. Got it."

Finn gave her shoulder a squeeze and walked over to the safe under the entertainment center. He entered a code and pulled the small heavy door open. Gathering up half a dozen healing potions and refilling any that were missing, Finn then gave two to Mila so she could do the same with the pockets on her corset harness. He gave the last two to Stephanie.

"These are healing potions. If you get hurt, pull the stopper and drink the whole thing. You have to drink the entire vial, or it won't work. Keep them safe, the vials are tough, but they can break."

Stephanie's eyes widened as he explained what they were. "Healing potions are real? Why don't we have these everywhere?"

Mila chuckled. "I asked the same thing. Turns out, they are crazy expensive, and the reagents are hard to produce. But don't hesitate to drink it if you need to. No amount of money is worth your life."

Finn checked to be sure Fragar was still in its holster, then patted down his pockets. His eyes widened in shock. "Oh, shit. I almost forgot."

He jogged into the kitchen, opened the freezer, and pulled out a fresh box of Charleston Chew Minis. He slipped them into his inside jacket pocket.

Mila threw up her hands. "We're going into battle. Why do you need candy?"

"Victory snack," Finn said confidently. He glanced out the window and saw the snowfall had increased to the point that he couldn't even make out the building across the street. As he watched, the wind began driving the snow sideways.

"This is going to suck," he said.

"I thought you didn't feel the cold? Stephanie and I will be freezing our tits off, but you should be fine."

"Oh, the cold isn't going to suck, the bad visibility means I won't be able to throw Fragar much." He glanced her way. "You're going to have a hell of a time using the Ivar."

Mila shook her head. "I'll just fire randomly. Bound to hit something."

Finn's jaw dropped, and she laughed.

"I'm kidding. Come on, I wouldn't do that." She stepped

up to him and grabbed him by the collar, her face sincere. "You be careful. You're not invincible. I need you to come home with us."

Finn leaned down, putting his forehead on hers, and looked into her eyes. "I'll do my best, darlin'."

She gave him a sad smile. "I suppose that's all any of us can do."

Mila tilted her head up and kissed him. They lingered like that for a few intimate moments before Stephanie cleared her throat while looking at the ceiling.

Finn laughed. "Okay, I get it. Sorry. You ready for this?"

Stephanie looked at Mila and smiled. "Yeah. Mila helped give me a pretty good foundation on how the world works. I know my mom has to be stopped, and that the darkness inside her drives her to insanity, but if it's at all possible, even a slim chance, can we show mercy to her?" Her wet gaze searched them both.

Finn's heart broke upon hearing her say that. He didn't see any way mercy was an option, but if there was a way to spare more lives, he would do his best. He had no idea what would happen to her afterward, but he guessed that wasn't really his problem.

"Like I told Mila, I'll do my best." He peered at both of them. "Let's do this."

Finn put a hand on Stephanie's right shoulder, and Mila did the same with her left. Stephanie pulled the clicker out of her pocket and put her finger over the button.

"Here we go," she said, clicking the button once.

Finn's phone rang, and he pulled it out with his free hand. Seeing the caller ID, he shouted. "Wait!"

Stephanie jumped a little but took her finger off the button.

"Preston? Hermin and Garret said your entire compound was destroyed."

"It was." Preston's smooth baritone was hoarse. "Luckily, we saw her coming on the long-distance surveillance. Most of my people got to the bunkers. Everything above ground is gone, just scraped the ground, but the bunkers held together. I'm assuming you're going after her?"

"We were just about to leave."

"Good. I have my G.A.E.L. teams standing by at an off-site facility. I need to know where to send them."

"We're not sure yet, just that it will be in town somewhere. I suggest you send your teams this way, and when I know where we are, I can get you a location."

Preston rumbled with pleasure. "That's a plan I can get behind. I'm sending them that way. They're at least twenty minutes out, depending on where you end up. Will that be too long?"

"Is there another option?"

"Well, that all depends on if she's using that thing that messes with magic. If it's off, they can teleport directly to you."

"I'll see what I can do. Thanks for the back up on this one."

"Hell, I still owe you for the last two." Preston gave a tired chuckle. "Be safe. That weapon is unimaginable."

The sound of multiple helicopters flying low roared over their building, making Finn jog to one of the broken out windows and glance up. He could just make out the dim silhouettes of a wave of Black Hawks flying past, followed by another wave, then a third.

"Are those your copters?" Finn asked into the phone when the engine roar abated.

"Not mine, and we haven't seen anything about the military dispatching people, as far as they know there's just some freak blizzard that hit Denver out of nowhere."

Finn's face hardened. "It must be her people."

"What direction were they headed?"

"Towards downtown, and at the rate they were moving, I would guess they'll be there in the next minute or two." Finn pulled back from the window and joining Stephanie and Mila.

"Okay. Get to it. The G.A.E.L. teams are *en route.* Good luck."

Finn hung up and put his phone in his pocket. "We should probably wait for them to land. I don't really fancy popping into a moving helicopter, or worse just outside of one."

The women nodded, and Finn pulled the Chews from his pocket, cracking the new box open, and offering some to Stephanie. "Chew while we wait?"

"Uh, sure. I've never seen these." She held out her hand, and he shook a few into her palm. "Are these, like, candy only old people know about, like Sugar Daddies and Black Jack Gum?"

Mila started laughing. "I call it manther food."

Finn cursed, and Mila doubled over with laughter.

"You two are weird," Stephanie said, cautiously biting into the tiny candy bar. "Hey, these are pretty good. I bet they would be awesome with coffee."

Mila stopped laughing and stared at her.

"Oh, look at that!" Finn shouted triumphantly. "I knew I liked her!"

## CHAPTER TWENTY-FIVE

Penny's eyes opened as she returned to consciousness. She found herself cradled in some kind of silk hammock that was pressing her into two firm, yet soft, heavy objects, each about the same size as she was if she were to curl into a ball. A few blinks and a head shake later, her vision cleared just enough to tell that the things she was pressed into were breasts. Danica's breasts to be precise. Penny didn't know they were Danica's because she knew what Danica's breasts looked like up close, but because they smelled like Danica.

To a dragon, everything was about smell. Even now, with the overpowering smell of Danica all around, Penny caught the scent of the fresh glacial water of Grand Lake just outside the house and knew that Finn had panicked once again and sent her and Danica off to "be safe" or some other sappy bullshit.

Penny tried to free herself from the makeshift baby sling Danica had put her in, but she was too weak for the second time that day, and it didn't help that Danica's boobs weighed as much Penny did. And that was individual weight; together? Forget about it.

*"Excuse me, hot-tits? Hello? I don't suppose you could let me out of the fucking baby sling, could you? Danica! Down here! Your boob is killing me!"* (Chi chi! Shir suqee!)

Danica moved at the sound of Penny's voice and pulled the sling open, exposing Penny's thin smile. Seeing her opportunity, she shot out of the sling at the first chance, ending up on Danica's somewhat precarious shoulder. Luckily for Penny, Danica was wearing a thick white sweater that was comfortable to hold onto. Unfortunately, Penny forgot that the sweater draped off of one shoulder, and it happened to be the one she chose.

Not wanting to scratch her friend—no matter how mad she was at her for agreeing to take her away from the fight—Penny flapped her wings, sending a burst of magic to them. She glided to the back of the couch. The dragon took a second to catch her breath, using what little magic she had left. They must have been close to the device Hellena used for it to have taken so much out of her.

Penny stretched her back and wings, standing up on her hind legs and reaching for the sky in a huge stretch that ended with her whipping her neck, just the way Finn hated and cracking each vertebra all the way up.

Right before that damned machine had turned on and knocked her out cold, Penny had caught snippets of the conversation Finn was trying to hide from Mila and the others. Hellena's part of the discussion was difficult to make out, but she had heard one thing that made all the pieces fall into place.

*Gjallarhorn.*

Penny almost slapped herself in the forehead out of shame when she had heard that. Penny saw the whole plan that crazy bitch had worked out in less than ten seconds, each thing leading to the next, and arriving at the Dark Star having a machine that warps magical fields so that the Gjallarhorn thinks she's a dwarven royal.

The plan was so simple, but it had an elegance to it that Penny had to admire. Penny chuckled. She had to admit, she had been giving that idiot *way* too much credit. Penny had been convinced it was some plan to wake up Peabrains by the thousands and use the resulting confusion to assert dominance.

Nope, it wasn't anything that involved. Turns out, the Dark Star just needed to figure out how to blow a stupid horn at people.

*"Is there anything to eat here? I need to replenish my magic."* (Shir?) Penny said, turning to see Danica staring at her with a blank look. Penny sighed. *"I'll check. Don't worry about it. I'm pretty sure the flight to the cupboards won't kill me. Fifty-fifty."* (chi shir.)

Penny launched off the couch and had a moment of panic when she fell out of the air, but she ended up on the far counter and able to stand on her hind legs to open and search the cupboards. The first one had half a bag of pretzels—that would do in a pinch—but Penny wasn't a fan. She went to the second cupboard and hit gold. Two boxes of Pop-Tarts, a S'mores and a Frosted Brown Sugar Cinnamon, her two favorites.

She hopped and knocked the S'mores box off the shelf and onto the counter, where she tore into it and slashed the Mylar wrapper open with a talon before pulling the pastry goodness to her mouth and taking a bite.

As soon as her saliva hit the sugary goodness, it broke the food down into magical energy. Penny felt a rush of power, filling her depleted reserves quickly, considering how processed Pop-Tarts were. The more natural the food, the more magic it contained, but Penny wasn't a fruit and veggie kind of girl. She liked processed junk and grilled meats. In all honesty, if someone gave her a salad and provided a paper napkin along with it, she would eat the napkin before the salad.

In two minutes, Penny ate the entire box of S'mores Pop-Tarts and was finishing off her first Brown Sugar Cinnamon when Danica approached her.

"Are you okay? You seem extra ravenous." She leaned a hip on the counter. "I know we don't talk much, I mean we literally can't talk, but I hope you know I brought you here because I wanted you to be safe. It was scary seeing you out like that. We all trust and rely on you so much..." she trailed off, biting at her thumbnail. "Well, I don't know what we would do without you."

Penny stopped eating, glanced at Danica, and gave her a small smile. She liked Danica. She was smart and strong-willed and stood by her friends even when it cost her an arm. That's bad-ass, and Penny appreciated Danica for all that, but what she really liked most about the elf was how freaking cute she could be. They had lived together for months, shared meals together, fought bad guys together, but she was still shy about expressing her feelings in a genuine, vulnerable way.

*"Girl, you need to own your shit! You are amazing. I mean,*

*first off, you're a fucking doctor. Kudos. Second, you look like a motherfucking supermodel, and you know it, but you don't act like it. Do you have any idea how hard that is to find? Third, you're dating the goofiest guy I have ever seen, and you're doing it because you like him as a person and don't give a flying fuck what other people think about it. I know you feel awkward around me because we can't really talk, and I know that's how you prefer to bond with people, but I need you.*

*"Look, I'll tell you a secret that no one else knows, not even Finn. You, Mila, and Finn... you three are the only people in the universe I'm willing to give my life for, and that puts me closer to my goal than I ever thought I would get. Now, that may not sound like a big deal to you, since it seems like every last one of you crazy bastards has a friend you would do that for, but I'm not like you. I'm a dragon. Dragons aren't the most friendly species, not to mention it's kinda part of our DNA to be greedy, selfish bastards. So, I realize you have no clue what I'm saying right now, and since I don't have a whole lot of options, I'm going to go against brand and give your stupid face a hug."* (Squee shee shir! Chi shee chi, shir.) Penny dropped the Pop-Tart and leaped onto the front of Danica's sweater, making the elf flinch, but also to instinctively catch her.

Penny scurried up until her neck was on the side of Danica's, and put her little arms around her neck and gave a firm squeeze. Penny had to hold the hug longer than she wanted to because it took Danica a few seconds to realize Penny wasn't attacking her. Once she understood, Penny felt her melt and hug her back.

"Penny, thank you. I've never seen you hug anyone before." Danica enjoyed the hug for a few more seconds before letting Penny lean back and look her in the eye. "I really wish I could understand you."

Penny gave her a half-smile and pointed a talon at herself, then held up two claws in a V shape.

Danica cocked her head, then comprehension dawned. "You too?"

Penny chuckled at Danica's excitement and nodded.

She hopped down to the counter and grabbed another package of processed pastries, then she flapped to the long wooden dining table by the floor-to-ceiling windows overlooking the frozen lake. Now that the Dark Star had left, and the spell she had put over the town to keep it empty was gone, the lake was covered in tents and portable sheds for ice fishing.

Penny needed to get back to the fight and to do that, she would need to cut off her magic. There was an ability her kind had that would work, but it was really a last-ditch effort kind of thing. If her kind ever found themselves hunted, then they could hide their magical presence, sealing it away. This had a few effects. The major one was that magic no longer affected them, which meant tracking spells couldn't find them. Magical attacks couldn't touch them; basically, they became a blank spot in the universe, and magic couldn't interact with them at all. But this had a secondary effect. The faerie dragon couldn't use their magic either. Just like magic was sealed out, it was also sealed in.

Faerie dragons are small, and not very tough without magic to back them up. Having her powers sealed away like that would mean that a good, solid stomp would end her. But she would be fine in the magical twisting area of effect.

She needed to be there. Finn would have figured it out as well, and he would try and solve it in a Finn way. He was going to destroy the device, and that would be worse than letting Hellena blow the damn horn. The magical feedback loop that would be created by destroying and releasing all that warped magic at the same time would blast a crater in the continent so big you could see it from the moon.

Penny couldn't let that happen.

She turned and motioned for Danica to join her. The elf pushed off the counter, bringing the last package of Pop-Tarts with her.

Penny mimicked using a phone, and Danica handed hers over before sitting down.

Danica narrowed her eyes as she opened the package and took a bite out of the pastry. "What's up?"

Penny opened the phone and selected a notepad app. She set the phone down so Danica could read it, then she started to type. Penny hated using words. They took so long to get out. She preferred magical speech. So many ideas could be compressed into a few sounds and gestures.

After what felt like forever, Penny showed Danica the phone, and waited while she read through the whole thing.

Danica sat back in her chair and blew a stray strand of hair out of her face. "You can actually block all incoming and outgoing magic?"

Penny nodded.

"And, you're saying that you can teach me how to tele-port, but you can't do it yourself?"

Again Penny nodded, and typed out "Not enough power. Don't channel magic, just store."

Danica seemed to understand this concept pretty well as she nodded along.

"Okay, and you're a hundred percent positive if you don't go back, Finn will smash this machine and blow up the entire state?"

Penny nodded.

Danica blew out a breath and collapsed onto the table-top, her head on its side so she was looking at Penny. "Fine. I believe you. Do it."

Penny walked over and patted her affectionately on the top of her head, before laying her left hand on Danica's temple and focusing her power.

Like what she did with Finn, when she took his emotions, she was doing with Danica. Except that instead of taking something away, like with Finn, this time, Penny was putting something *in* Danica's head. The knowledge of a spell Penny had never been able to do but learned anyway—just in case.

Turns out this *was* the case. And it had become a 'just-in' scenario.

# CHAPTER TWENTY-SIX

Stephanie clicked the button a third time. Finn blinked, and the condo vanished in a flash of red and black swirling colors. Finn blinked again and the swirling reds and blacks resolved into a path-strewn park. They found themselves standing on a lawn with only a thin covering of snow, next to a row of shrubs strung with white decoration lights hanging in their snow-dusted branches.

Finn directed them to crouch and use the hedges as cover while he surveyed the area. He recognized it as Capitol City Park, a strip of meticulously cared for land that was bookended by the Denver courthouse, and the Colorado capital building. Several monuments dotted the park, along with a geometric pattern of walkways and fountains. Most of those features were overshadowed, however, by the chaos all around them.

Finn's mouth dried as he saw the power on display, both magical and mundane. He counted over a dozen Black Hawks parked haphazardly across the lawn, their engines off, but still radiating heat waves, along with thirty or more black motorcycles and SUVs. Soldiers were standing in groups, some armed to the teeth with automatic rifles and body armor, along with several that appeared to have only sidearms, but had the look of attack mages. Most magical races were present at a glance, all the more easy to spot since they tended to gather with others of their ilk.

In the center of it all, and only twenty or so feet away from them, was a two-foot cube made of black metal panels covered in red, glowing runes. A generator had been wired up to it with thick, black, electrical cables. It was apparent the machine had not been switched on yet. Its display screen, attached to the side of the cube, was powered down.

Next to the machine, Finn spied the Gjallarhorn.

It was a bit smaller than he imagined the legendary relic might be. At nearly three feet long, an actual animal horn had been coated in an intricate pattern of gold, silver, and Mythril. Finn recognized sigils from his family heraldry worked into designs that sent an inexplicable chill down his spine.

The horn itself sat in a stainless steel metal stand holding it aloft at head height so the user could blow it while not having to bear the weight of the heavy instrument.

Hellena, the Dark Star, stood behind the Gjallarhorn in all her dark splendor. Her face had healed from the blast of celestial magic Mila had delivered on the lake, but there seemed to be a tightness to her left cheek still as if the skin were just a little too taut to fit comfortably. Despite the slight defect, she was still beautiful, with long raven black hair, and piercing eyes that seemed to look directly through you. She wore a black, felt gown with long sleeves and a short train that flowed out behind her a foot or so. Her throat and collarbone were exposed to the cold by a plunging neckline, but her skin showed no redness or signs of chill.

Black smoke roiled around her, pooling at her feet, and rising above her head and shoulders like a cowl. That smoke had been present the last time Finn had seen her, but now it seemed thicker and more substantial. A sign that Finn recognized as her falling deeper into the darkness consuming her.

However, the most extraordinary thing about it all was that while a blizzard of biblical proportions raged all around them, there was a circle that encompassed the entire park, along with the front facades of the government buildings at each end, where no snow was falling. The wall of white powder slithered around the cylinder of calm like a giant snake, seeing its prey inside a glass jar and seeking its way in.

Then, there was the snow thunder.

Finn had seen a lot of shit in his life, but never had he seen anything like this. The blizzard was lit from within as lightning bolts flashed through the storm, one after another, the snow refracting the light and spreading it out so that whole sections glowed with angry energies as light bounced around, trapped in the snowstorm. The sound of thunder was constant, but only just audible, the thick snow absorbing almost all the noise.

Finn quickly hit the talk button on his earpiece and spoke softly. "Remmy, I hope you're ready because this is going to be a hell of a shit show. We're at the Capitol City Park. Get word to the Huldu and Preston if you can. I don't exactly have time to make a phone call."

The goblin's raspy voice cut in. "We're on our way, Boss. I'll let the others know. Try and stall 'em. We have more minutes before we get there. Not many." The line went quiet, and Finn muted his end.

A group of Kashgar noticed them first, raising the alarm with a shout, and leveling rifles and hands that filled with bubbles of magic.

Hellena regarded them with a cold smile. "Kill them," she ordered, before noticing Stephanie standing behind Finn. "Hold!"

The men seemed a little confused but lowered their weapons and hands slightly. The call had garnered the attention of several groups close by and they all came running, their guns at the ready, but held in check for the time being.

Hellena's dark expression faded as she looked at her daughter. Stepping closer, Hellena spread her arms out, her face almost beatific with joy. "Stephie. Oh, I've missed you so much. Come, give me a hug."

Finn felt Stephanie grab hold of the back of his jacket and move closer to him, half hiding from her mother.

Hellena's demeanor changed in an instant. "I said come here, child."

"No." Stephanie started weakly, but she gained volume and confidence with each new word. "I don't even know who you are. My mother would never do this."

The outrage changed again, this time to disgust. "You're right. That weak woman had no drive. I made her better, more powerful, more resilient. Your mother was weak, so I reforged her. Come and join me, child, and I shall do the same for you."

"You're insane," Stephanie said in disbelief. "I wanted to save you; to bring you back, but I don't even know if you're still there."

Hellena struggled with herself, her teeth clenched and eyes rolling wildly. She finally calmed and the face Finn saw shocked him. She had fear in her eyes.

"Oh, my poor girl. I'm so sorry, I was just trying to protect you, not control you. I wanted a normal life for you, not one mired in magical politics."

"So you locked my powers away, and made me tell people that creep was my dad? How is that making things better for me? You abandoned me. When I turned fifteen, you left for six months. Do you know what it's like to live alone at fifteen? It's terrifying. You did that to me. My life isn't better. Look around. You think this is a good life?"

"Life isn't easy, Stephie." Hellena was becoming more wooden in her movements. "Sometimes, it gets messy. There are a lot of people that need help; that need protecting, and I thought I could be the one to provide it." She clenched her teeth, obviously in pain. Her eyes screwed shut. "I just needed a little more power."

Hellena's face relaxed, and she opened her eyes. They had become solid black orbs, the blue was gone. Blood trickled from her tear ducts, leaving red lines down her cheeks. She smiled. "Lucky for me I found all the power I could ever want."

"You were supposed to protect *me* first." Stephanie cried, clutching at Finn's jacket as a sob racked her. "Now, you're no better than a monster." Stephanie buried her face into the back of Finn's jacket, wracked with sobs.

The Dark Star pursed her lips in disgust at the show of emotion. "I'm done with this. No daughter of mine could ever be this weak. Kill them all." She turned and walked towards the Gjallarhorn. Her men took aim and fired.

# CHAPTER TWENTY-SEVEN

"**B**alla cloiche."

Finn set his magic free. He crouched and drew Fragar. A wall of stone two feet thick and ten feet long shot out of the ground, rising to just over three feet high and blocking the incoming bullets and spells. Chunks of the wall rained down around him, but he could feel it was stable and would hold.

A muttered word and Fragar unfolded, blazing with purple magic and itching for a fight. Finn glanced down the wall and saw Mila had pulled out the Ivar. She was keeping cover and looking at him, then at Stephanie. "We need to keep her safe."

Finn nodded and pulled the young woman around in front of him. He took her by the shoulders and resisted hugging her tight, Hellena's last words sounding so similar to the words his father had last said to him.

"I'm going to put you in a stone fortress. I can't protect you otherwise." He said, keeping his voice calm as his rage began to flow in his blood.

She nodded, and he sat her down on the ground, placing a hand in the snow and focusing. "This won't take long, then we'll have a hot coffee and talk it all out." He reached into his inside jacket pocket and tossed her the Charleston Chews. "Just in case you get hungry." He gave her a wink.

"*Daingneach.*"

He forced power through himself, and the earth reacted. A granite square three feet thick with an opening just large enough to fit Stephanie rose quickly around her, stopping when it reached six feet. It wasn't perfect, but it would have to do. He doubted that anyone would try to climb in during a fight, and it was going to be a hell of a dispute.

Mila poked her head around the end of the wall to aim and unleashed a white blast of energy from the Ivar. The celestial bolt tore through three men, before slamming into a Black Hawk. The chopper exploded and tumbled through the air. It landed on four orcs that happened to be charging at the wrong time.

"Aim for the machine, we need to neutralize the horn," Finn shouted, spinning as three Kashgar came around the end of the wall. The one in the lead had full-body armor on, Fragar sliced through it as if it were a tee-shirt. The man's scream became a gurgle as his damaged lungs filled with blood.

The two behind were casters, and they lobbed small bubbles that burst into flame. Finn smacked the first away with the flat of his ax and sidestepped the second. He charged forward, his rage awakened. His steps quickened and he had decapitated the first Kashgar before the latter could form another bubble.

To the man's surprise, Finn didn't chop his ax at him; instead he snatched the back of his collar and spun him to face his fellows, who didn't seem to have any trouble mowing him down to get to Finn.

Charging forward, the bullet-riddled Kashgar shield held high, Finn closed the distance with the nearest group and lobbed their dead fellow at them before tearing like a dervish into the tight cluster of Kashgar.

---

"Aim for the machine, we need to neutralize the horn," Finn shouted, before turning and slicing a man in half.

Mila watched him for a second, before glancing around the stone wall Finn had summoned from the ground and searched for the cube.

A flash of orange light coming in from her left caught her attention, and she ducked back behind the wall as a fireball splashed across the corner she'd been peeking around. Some of the brining liquid fire splashed on her boot, and she twisted her leg to smother the small flame in the snow and dirt. When she looked up, the caster, an elf woman whose face was contorted with rage, loomed over her, an angry red glow forming between her palms.

Mila pointed the pistol up and fired from the hip, the thick bolt of white-hot power incinerating the elf's hands, arms, and head. The rest of the body fell at her feet, but Mila didn't have time to be horrified at the sight as she scrambled to her knees and popped up, the Ivar held in two hands. She pulled the trigger, sending another bolt of pure magic racing for the black cube.

Mila smiled. "That was easy."

Her smile faded when the bolt of white light slammed into a barrier of black smoke and dissipated, leaving the cube untouched.

"Oh, I'm all studied up on your particular brand of magic, Valkyrie." Hellena sneered, before throwing her hand out and sending half a dozen black spikes streaking towards Mila.

Pushing off the wall, Mila was able to roll backward and avoid the spikes, which passed over her only to slam into an orc's chest. She was clear of the first attack, but the move had thrown her outside the protective cover of the wall.

Before she could react, a black bolt, not much different from Mila's white bolt, slammed into her chest, her armor taking most of the blow, but it still threw her off her feet to tumble through the snow and slide to a stop on her back.

She was exposed to a group of soldiers that had come running when the fighting started but was just now getting into range. They raised their guns and two of them threw bubbles, one popping into a green acid, and the other turning into an ice spike.

Mila scrambled and let out a scream when she saw she wasn't going to be fast enough to avoid the attack.

---

Finn heard Mila scream as he cut down the last of the Kashgar. He spun about to find her. His rage was full bore, his vision red at the edges, but he also kept up his mantra that he was in control, not the blood. So far, it worked.

He had been hit with a force bubble that blew the shoulder off of his jacket, but he had taken hardly any damage at all. Right after that, he had sent a stone spike through two charging men, and his control was spot on.

Now that Mila was in trouble, he allowed the rage to have the upper hand. He spotted her, just as the casters sent their bubbles her way. He roared in anger at not being able to do anything to stop them, then he paused when he saw the earth quickly mound up in the path of the spells, catching them both and letting them either soak in or shatter depending on the spell type.

Finn blinked in confusion but didn't have long to consider when a bullet ripped through his left forearm and pulled his attention to a group hunkering down around a monument ten yards away.

He pivoted, and charged, weaving in an unpredictable pattern, and causing both bullets and spells to miss, if only by fractions of an inch. At the last second, he spun like a wide receiver and attacked the right side of the monument instead of the left where he had focused his snarling insults as he had run.

Coming in with an overhand chop, Fragar bit into a Peabrain's head, cleaving the entire back of the skull off without slowing. Finn lowered his shoulder and hacked the next guy in the gut, then he bull-rushed through six men, knocking three to the ground, and slicing the legs off one of the others. Finn kicked out with his right leg, catching another in the groin, and tumbled to the ground with him, their limbs tangled.

Finn buried Fragar in the man's chest then pulled it free and threw it at the last man standing. Finn didn't even check to see if the ax hit its mark, trusting in his abilities; instead, he scooped up a rifle as he sprang to his feet and smashed it into the face of one of the three he'd bowled over.

Running past the monument, Finn ripped Fragar free of the chest of the man he had thrown it at and shouted, "*Spìc cloiche*," while channeling magic into the ground. The sound of spikes ripping through the last two men told Finn he hadn't missed with the magic either.

The fight only took a few seconds, but when Finn ran to where Mila had been laid out, he was shocked to see a mound of dirt rising eight or nine feet tall and humanoid-shaped. It appeared to be made of packed dirt with stones and twigs mixed in giving it a lumpy, unfinished look. It blinked glowing yellow eyes, surveying the scene before pointing at Finn.

"Dwarf?" The giant thing's voice sounded like Barry White had eaten a bag of rocks and every rumbling word crushed the rocks to dust.

"Yeah. Dirt Elemental?"

"Yeah."

That seemed to be the extent of the exchange. Dirt focused his attention on Hellena. "You must stop. Earth wants your darkness gone."

Hellena, unlike most of the others around, didn't seem all that phased by the sight of the towering brute. She smirked. "You think I give a shit what this old ship wants? You want me to stop? Come make me."

Dirt started a ponderous run that took him directly at

the group of soldiers that had been attacking Mila. With a swipe of his arm, he sent the entire group flying off into the night, their screams cut off as they hit the ground. The Elemental didn't stop his run however, and Finn realized the only reason he had even attacked the men was because they happened to be between him and the Dark Star.

With each step, Dirt picked up speed, each footfall shaking the ground. Soon his footsteps were coming fast enough it was difficult for Finn to keep his footing. He saw several people fall over, and no one was able to fight in the earthquake-like tremors.

Finn saw the Dark Star reach down and flip a switch on the machine, and the red runes grew in intensity. The device whined with some internal mechanism spinning on an axis.

Dirt stumbled, slowing down, then falling to a knee. To Finn's shock, the elementals arm fell off at the elbow.

Dirt looked up at the Dark Star, his face a mask of pain. "You can't win."

"Looks like I already have, rocks for brains."

Finn was trying to figure out a way to get the damned machine off, but with Hellena hovering over it…

His thoughts were cut off when all the trees in the park began to shake, dislodging their snow in huge white puffs. As he watched, all the trees leaned towards the Elemental like there was some calm wind sucking them to him.

Finn had to cover his eyes when the sky lit up with raw magic that began to flow in giant rivers from the trees and into the Elemental. The lost arm was reabsorbed into his foot, while at the same time, a new arm grew from the stump. With a ground-shaking move, Dirt climbed to his feet and roared in defiance at Hellena, her hair being blown back from the wind.

When he quieted, she smiled pleasantly, her black eyes showing no emotion. "My turn."

She sucked in a breath and blew the Gjallarhorn.

The note started low and quickly rose, ending in a tearing sound as the universe was ripped open for a split second. Raw energy blasted out from the tear and engulfed the Dirt Elemental along with half a dozen of the Dark Star's men. The blast of power only lasted a fraction of a second, but as it dissipated the destruction was clear. Nothing remained of the Elemental except scattered pebbles. The men were converted to red mist, and the ground was scraped clean all the way across the park. Even part of the courthouse's facade crumbled from the short note.

Finn knew he had to stop this woman. No one should have that kind of power, especially someone as insane as her. He let the rage flow, gripping Fragar in two hands and roaring.

She looked over at him with boredom in her eyes. "You want a turn, as well?"

Finn broke into a sprint, closing the distance in a matter of moments. His vision was almost entirely red, but he held tight to that last little thread of humanity making sure he had a way back.

Hellena didn't bother using the horn again. Instead, she flicked a hand upward, sending out a wall of thick black smoke.

Finn didn't hesitate and charged into the smoke wall, passing through it as it left a burning sensation on his skin and his clothes smoking. Her look of surprise made the discomfort worth it. He smashed his ax down in a two-handed overhead blow, but she was able to block it by creating a shield of condensed black smoke that became as solid as steel. In her other hand, she created a sword of the same material and swung it at his guts, forcing him to dance backward or be sliced open. They exchanged blows, and Finn was surprised at her skill, but he could tell that he was better than her. He just needed to wait for the right moment.

She backed him up a good ten feet when he saw her starting to tire, and he knew his moment was coming. When she dropped her guard, a loud *popping* sound came from behind Finn, and he was forced to spin away or be trapped between Hellena and one of her casters.

Preparing to fight on two fronts, Finn turned so that he could see both enemies, but he stopped, his rage-clouded mind having trouble understanding what was happening.

The Dark Star had fled to the Gjallarhorn, and where there should have been another enemy, Danica stood there with Penny in her arms.

Finn snapped his head to the side and saw Hellena taking a deep breath, preparing to blow the horn at him and take Danica and Penny out in the process. Finn let the rage take him, but instead of listening to it as it demanded him to go after the Dark Star, he turned to Danica and wrapped her and Penny up in his arms and forced them to the ground so Danica was sitting between his legs, her body curled down against him so that none of her was in line with the horn.

"What?" Was all Danica got out before the note

sounded, and Finn roared his defiant reply. A pain unlike anything Finn had ever felt tore into his back, but he could tell that for every bit of magic that took hold and tried to rip him from the world, there was an ocean's worth he was able to ignore.

Danica was screaming, but that meant she was still alive, so Finn reveled in that scream as he endured the Gjallarhorn's ministrations. It felt like an eternity, even knowing the blast was only a fraction of a second long, but it did eventually stop. He felt the cold winter air slam into his bloody and raw back like a pick to stone. And he gasped in pain.

"What the hell was that?" Danica said, shakily lifting her head and looking at him.

"You made it," he said drunkenly. " I think there's something wrong with my back."

Danica took a quick look and came back with a pale drawn look on her face. She swallowed. "Where are your healing potions?"

Finn reached for the potions on his holster, but all that was left were a few scraps of leather in his lap. "Gone."

Holding out a hand Danica focused her magic, imbuing him with healing power, but the machine was still on, and the spell came out as a green slime that coated his chest.

# CHAPTER TWENTY-EIGHT

On one shaky knee, Finn turned toward the cackle, keeping Danica behind him.

The Dark Star stood behind the horn, laughing like a maniac. "I can't believe you survived that, dwarf! You are truly an aberration. No matter, all I have to do is keep hitting you. You're not immune, just exasperatingly persistent."

Hellena took a deep breath to blow a death knell when a flash drew her attention. She looked to the side as a white-hot bolt from Mila's gun came from the left. The Dark Star's magic countered the blast, and she sent a spear of black energy back.

Finn struggled to get to his feet but failed. His back, a mess of shredded bone and gristle exposed through flesh, kept him down. He roared in pain and rage, but all he could do is watch as the lance of blackness rushed towards Mila.

"Nooo!"

In a truly Mila move, she didn't dodge. Instead, she

fired the Ivar again. The two bolts met in the air, and with a thunderous, sizzling crack they canceled each other out.

Finn seethed and struggled to his feet.

"Finn, careful!" Danica said, grabbing at his arm.

"She needs me," he yelled.

A scream from more than a dozen yards away caught everyone's attention, and Finn saw one of Hellena's soldiers fall from a bloody wound to the leg. Then another went down, and another.

Finn laughed aloud, catching Hellena's attention. Beside him, Danica smiled, understanding why Finn had turned joyous.

The Dark Star bared her teeth at him and lowered her brows over her blood-filled eyes. "What are you laughing at, you pathetic creature?"

Finn pointed. "Reinforcements."

A group of soldiers seemed to fight off an invisible enemy. Then, a beefy, male goblin popped into view when his inherent ability to turn invisible timed out and needed to reset. Another goblin appeared, followed by a dozen more. All of them were dressed in variations of street clothes, but with armor pieces strapped to them and holding long curved knives that gleamed wickedly in the lightning storm.

"We're here, Boss," Remmy said in his earpiece. "We have your back, now take the Star bitch out."

More shouting from behind made Finn and Hellena shift focus to the other side of the park as a hail of bullets tore from the wall of the raging blizzard. It cut down a confused group of orcs and elves that had been running to help with the new goblin threat.

Coming out of the snow, dressed in full tactical gear and moving in coordinated cover, Preston's G.A.E.L. teams arrived in four groups of heavily armed and armored men and women from all races. They moved from the raging storm, firing on targets.

Most of the Dark Star's people hadn't been in the fight up to this point, having been ordered to keep anyone out, and therefore not all charging in when Finn and Mila started fighting. The Dark Star's army, with over a hundred soldiers, now found themselves in for a real fight.

The G.A.E.L. squads and Remmy's tribe helped even the odds, though still in the Dark Star's favor in terms of numbers. Finn had to remind himself this battle was far from won. That didn't mean he wouldn't stall for time by talking crazy amounts of shit.

"Oh, look," Finn said, gesturing towards the G.A.E.L. troopers. "I guess you missed a few people when you tried to sneak attack Preston's place. Sloppy work, Hellena."

A smile slowly spread across her face, the bloody tears and black eyes making the expression a twisted parody. "Don't you get it? This is what I want. Here I thought I would have to bring the war to them, but they came to me. How considerate." The smile dropped from her face. "Now, I just take care of you, and I'm free to tear the city down around us. The damage will be far more than a little blizzard can hide. Within a day, every news channel on Earth will be showing magicals fighting in the streets with Peabrains. At that point, all I have to do is sit back and watch. Once the magical community knows they don't have to hide anymore, forming our own nation is the next logical step. We will be the new world superpower and every country will bend the knee!"

Movement out of the corner of Finn's eye caught his attention. At a glance, he felt his heart leap for joy. The tiny blue form of Penny hunkered in the shadow of the machine. She had an almost glossy sheen that covered her from head to toe. It let off tiny wisps of blue and red vapor that vanished within inches of leaving her body.

Penny had her eyes on Hellena, making sure she wasn't seen, but she was slowly unscrewing a panel on the black cube, trying to get access to the guts of the machine. Penny caught him glancing at her, and she smiled.

Danica also noticed Penny. "Finn…"

"I know. Keep behind me," he said.

Finn gave Penny a barely perceptible nod, and the dragon knew he was going to keep Hellena busy for her. She turned her attention to opening the panel, and the work went faster.

"That's your great plan?" Finn called out in a mocking tone. "Just start a war and hope for the best? You sound like my father."

"You've seen the way the magicals are forced to be second-hand citizens out of fear of discovery. Always afraid that they'll be found out, and ruin it for the rest of our secret society. Who cares if they find out. We have fucking magic on our side. The foolish Peabrains should lick our boots out of gratitude we didn't subjugate them after Alexandria. Such pathetic creatures! Our place is not behind concealment spells and living in sewers. Our place is at the top. We *will* win this war, and when a new nation is formed, one that can stand against all, people like you will thank me for the sacrifices I made. Why do you insist on fighting me when you *know* I'm right?"

Finn grinned, but it turned to a grimace as a wave of pain washed over his back. "You're right. It's not fair how magicals are repressed. You're also right that in a stand-up fight, the Peabrains would lose. But those are not reasons to kill a billion people in a globe-spanning war. I've struggled with you and your idea from the beginning. I value freedom, especially my own, above most things, and on paper what you want to accomplish, I agree with."

Hellena smiled a triumphant smile at that admission.

"However," Finn added, holding up a finger, "there is one major problem with your plan. While you might be right, that doesn't make you a leader. Being right isn't good enough; you have to be just. You can't say you want to give people freedom then throw lives at the problem and hope for the best. You have to fight tooth and nail to be sure the highest number of your people get to enjoy that freedom too."

Finn waved a hand around the battlefield as her soldiers died or killed in her name. "You don't care about them. If you did, you wouldn't have been standing by while they were being killed, you would have been in the fight. These people who follow you because you sold them the dream of freedom, will never get to know its embrace because you're using them as meat shields."

Hellena's face had gone from angry to happy to confused then ended back at angry. Finn had almost laughed watching the rollercoaster of emotion he had taken her on. He wasn't even sure what he had said, he was just trying to buy time for Penny.

"I'm going to enjoy killing you, Finnegan. You are so full of shit I almost believe *you* believe the shit you say. Power begets power. If you want to make it in this world, you better have the power to keep yourself moving, because time and again, Peabrains have chewed us up and spat us out."

Hellena sucked in a breath and aimed the Gjallarhorn. Finn pushed Danica behind him as Hellena put her lips to the mouthpiece. Stephanie appeared and slid to a stop in front of Finn and Danica, her arms spread wide.

"Please, mom. Please stop. This is sick. There has to be a better way. Just come back to me." She sniffed. "I need you to come back. I need my mom back."

Hellena hesitated, and for a moment, Finn saw her eyes flash from black to blue, but then her face hardened and without a word, blew a long note.

Finn grimaced and wrapped his arms around Stephanie and Danica, expecting the worst, but the note ended, and nothing changed. Hellena looked confused and blew another blast on the instrument. Again, the flesh was not peeled from Finn's body—or anyone else's.

Hellena's head jerked to the side. She howled when she saw Penny backing out of an access panel in the cube, a circuit board in her hand, wires attached to it having been bitten through to separate it from its place in the machine.

Hellena, aided by her dark magic, was fast, and lunged for Penny, her hand outstretched and teeth snarling. Penny, even with her magic sealed away, was quick. The dragon darted around the cube, running halfway to Finn before throwing the vital part of the machine to him.

Finn caught the circuit board and crushed it in one

hand, while Penny whirled around and gave double middle fingers to Hellena.

Throwing her head back, the Dark Star screamed into the night air. The black smoke surrounding her saw its opening to take more control, and seized upon it, wrapping her from head to toe in thick tendrils, allowing the barest outline of Hellena to show through.

Finn felt Danica's hands slap against his back. Making him cry out as pain coursed through his damaged body. Just as he was about to pull away, he felt healing energy flow through him. Danica's hands became warm and soothing pools on his ravaged flesh, as he felt the muscle and skin close up.

Breathing deep, Finn endured the mix of pain and pleasure as he was healed, focusing on his breathing, and maintaining his heart rate as the rage fought for dominance in him.

As quickly as it had begun, it was over. Danica ran her hands over his newly healed back, checking for any malformations, then slumped to the ground, catching her breath.

Finn turned to see she was smiling and giving him a thumbs-up.

"Thank you," he said, gently touching her cheek before rising to stand by Stephanie.

She backed into him, her hand over her mouth. "What is happening to her?" she whispered.

"The darkness is taking her, molding her to its purpose. I'm sorry. There's nothing I can do to save her." He put his hand on her shoulder.

"I can do something," Mila said, running to him, and

throwing her arms around his neck and squeezing hard. "I thought you were a dead man."

"Where have you been? I've been worried sick." Finn rumbled, letting her slip to the ground.

"Sorry, ran into a pack of elves, and had to take care of business." She smiled, then looked over at the changing body in the twisting smoke chrysalis. "I can save her."

"It's not possible. She's far too gone," Finn argued, watching as Hellena's fingers grew in length, to form into talons.

"I can do it." She put a hand on his cheek. "Trust me."

"Always." He looked to see Hellena had grown in height by six inches. "You better not be wrong."

"I'm not." Mila stepped back, giving his hand a squeeze before turning to Stephanie. "Don't worry. I've got this."

Finn pulled Stephanie to where Danica was sitting up, still breathing hard. He watched as the love of his life took off at a jog towards the Dark Star—all alone.

"Penny? Can you fight?" Finn asked, looking at the small dragon.

She shook her head and made a sad noise.

"It's okay, my friend. Stay with them, okay? I'm going to back Mila up. If she's going to do what I think she is, she's going to be vulnerable. You three get somewhere safe and keep your heads down."

He didn't wait for an answer; instead, he jogged after Mila, ripping the tattered remains of his black teeshirt off as he went.

The Dark Star's transformation sped up, and Finn felt a spike of panic.

Mila raced towards the smoke-shrouded figure, her

arms outstretched ready to wrap the creature in an embrace. When Mila was three steps from the Dark Star, there was a ripping sound as the creature in the chrysalis tore free.

With a casual backhand, the Dark Star hit Mila in the chest, jettisoning her backward and over Finn's head to land beside Danica, her arms obviously broken and blood pouring from her mouth.

# CHAPTER TWENTY-NINE

Finn's world turned red with rage. He launched himself at the thing and chopped down with Fragar. A black-taloned hand batted the blade to the side but had to back up a step or be sliced by the return swing.

They moved at incredible speed, attacking and parrying blow after blow. Finn's sheer manic energy was pushing him hard, and he was gaining ground, then two blades were formed from the remaining smoke and began to attack independently of the Dark Star, as they floated beside her, chopping and slashing at his exposed parts.

Finn was driven back, fighting what was essentially three opponents at once. He did his best, as the blades clanged and sparked off of Fragar, yet he continued to backpedal to keep out of reach of her talons.

Taking one more step backward, Finn half-stepped on a small curb around a planter and lost his balance. It was only for a moment, but it was enough for one of the blades to slice into his right arm.

Pain erupted in the wound like molten metal poured

into his veins. He blocked another floating sword strike, but took a blow to the stomach that knocked the wind out of him, and dropped him onto his ass. He did his best to block the next hit, but the sword hooked itself in Fragar's hooked tip and was able to pull the ax from his hands. He watched in dread as it tumbled through the air and landed twenty feet away.

He looked up and noticed that the Dark Star's eyes had gone from black to red. It was a curious detail he hadn't seen before. It gave her elongated face a devilish feel.

The two swords floated over her head and joined as one giant blade. She reached up, taking it in both hands and grinning. Blood dripped from her mouth and splattered on the ground between Finn's legs.

Screaming like a banshee, the Dark Star chopped down with all her might.

Mila slipped in between him and the Dark Star, like the last dancer between the curtains, and taking a knee, held her arm up in a defensive stance. Finn began to bellow in rage and despair, yet when the black sword smashed down on her arm, a shield of white and gold light appeared. It looked as though she were encased in a bubble, but only the part affected by the blade was visible at any given time.

The Dark Star smashed the sword down again. The celestial shield rebuffed the attack.

Mila looked over her shoulder at him and smiled, tossing an empty healing potion to the ground.

"You need to get the hell out of here, Mila. That thing is way stronger than I thought."

She shook her head, grunting as another blow rained

down. "And leave my hero defenseless? I thought you knew me better than that."

Unfortunately, he did know her better than that.

"Penny!" Mila called, "Get a healing potion to Finn. There's something wrong with his arm."

Finn looked down and was shocked to see that his right arm was nothing but a withered husk from the bicep down. He stared in shock until Penny pressed a healing potion into his hand, and he gulped it down. The wither stopped, but the arm remained deformed.

Mila let out a pained grunt and had to use her free hand to steady her.

Finn was desperately trying to figure out a way to get Mila out of the way, but with the Dark Star's blows coming so fast, he didn't see how it was possible.

That was when the ground behind the Dark Star shuddered and rose up.

"About fucking time," Mila grunted.

The Dirt Elemental rose from the ground, his proportions much larger than before. He stopped when he was waist height and still towered fifteen feet into the air. He ponderously raised his arms, his hands splayed and overly large, even for their current overgrown size.

The Dark Star realized they were looking behind her. She stopped slamming the sword against Mila's shield and turned to see the giant's hands clapping together around her.

With a *boom*, Dirt's hands slammed together, cutting off all view of the Dark Star.

Finn and Mila took a deep breath of relief. Then Dirt's hand began to flex and strain.

"She's digging out," Dirt boomed.

Mila gave Finn a smile. "Love you, babe. Be back in a minute."

Before he could stop her, she charged at Dirt's hands and shouted, "Open up!" when she was two steps away.

Dirt pulled his hands away as she closed in, revealing a dazed Dark Star. Mila opened her arms and tackled Hellena to the ground…where they froze in place.

# CHAPTER THIRTY

Mila stumbled back from the frozen, twisted form of Hellena, and cupped her hands to amplify her voice. "Victoria! I need help."

After a few seconds, the tall blonde woman appeared, this time barefoot and in pajamas.

"What the hel...what the fuck is that?" she said, looking at the monster.

"That's the Dark Star," Mila said dismissively, moving the conversation along. "You said that the Reaper can change a soul. Can it separate dark magic from regular magic?"

"Dark magic did this? I don't think I've ever seen someone get this far along. They usually die." Victoria scrutinized the bloodied creature. "Yes, the Reaper can do what you want, but remember the cost is very high."

"How high?" Mila had considered saying she didn't care, but that would have been a lie. There was only so much she would be willing to pay. Even if it was to give Stephanie her mother back.

"You will not be able to use the Reaper again until you can return here. After you reap a soul, the average time it takes to return is ten years."

Mila nodded. "Okay, so far. What else?"

Victoria frowned. "That's it. Isn't that enough?"

"I'm missing something. That doesn't sound that bad."

"I forget you have no knowledge. This will make it even worse for you. Because we can come here, we can interact with one another, teach each other, and spend time with our sisters. Without access to this place, we become Lone Valkyries. Our powers still work, and we have access to our magic, but we cannot be near another Valkyrie or we both become weak and vulnerable. You must walk the earth apart from the sisterhood, and endure until you are welcomed back into the fold."

"Okay, that sounds a little worse than I thought, but I'm going to say it's still worth it." Mila looked over at the tortured soul she had brought and thought about Stephanie and her anguish. "Bring me the Reaper."

"It's already here," Victoria said.

Mila turned and the woman had a large thin wooden case in her arms held out so Mila could open it. She lifted the bronze latch and then raised the lid slowly and reverently.

She was surprised to see a rather plain-looking hand scythe. It was made of a rust-brown metal with a worn wooden handle. While everything about the scythe looked like something you find in a hundred-year-old barn, the blade was honed to a mirrors finish with an edge so sharp Mila couldn't see where the metal ended and the air began.

"Go on. You must wield it," Victoria prompted.

Mila carefully picked the scythe up, amazed at how light it was. "How do I use it?"

Victoria smiled. "Like a scythe. Just reap her soul. The work comes after."

Mila stepped up to the Dark Star, frozen and helpless, and almost felt sorry for her. Before she could give it much thought, she swung the blade through Hellena's chest. There was no resistance as if there was no flesh at all, and when she looked closely, there was no blood either. There was, however, a waving tendril of vaporous material waving off of her like a little flag.

"Now, we harvest," Victoria said. "Begin pulling the soul out of the body. This part can take a minute." She willed a chair into existence and plopped down.

Mila grasped the wisp between two fingers and pulled. It was an odd sensation not feeling the thing you are touching, but evidently, souls were either wholly insubstantial, or they just felt like nothing.

After a few minutes of pulling, Mila understood why Victoria had summoned a chair. This was *really* going to take a minute.

---

Finn was doing his best to fight off those that could come to their master's rescue, but with only one arm, he was off balance and getting sloppy from tiredness.

It had been nearly twenty minutes since Mila had taken Hellena wherever it was she could go, and Finn had been fighting the entire time. He was ready to drop but knew he couldn't leave Mila undefended, so he pushed harder.

Bodies littered the ground around him, and he was coated in blood, which to Finn's relief was evidently gruesome enough that some of the soldiers were turning away, widely thinking it wasn't worth their life.

However, it looked like his luck was running out as a group of seven elves spotted him and charged.

With a weary sigh, he hefted Fragar in his good hand and set himself for battle once again. They closed in, hands up and forming bubbles, and a few pulling out knives.

Just before they all let loose, their expressions changed from anger to confusion, then to horror, as they all slowed their run to a jog, then to a standstill.

"Are we doing this, or what guys? I'm pretty tired, so if we could just hurry this along?" Finn said as politely as he could but felt it was still a little *dickish*.

The elf closest to him held up a hand and realized he was holding a knife that he dropped. "Uh, excuse me. Could you tell me where we are, exactly? And maybe why there are dead people everywhere?"

Finn's brows rose. A gasp from behind made him spin and take a knee, helping Mila to sit up.

"Are you okay?" he asked.

She nodded, coughing a few times. "I'm good. I did it. I cut the darkness out of her."

Another gasp and Hellena sat up, her eyes wide with fear. "What is happening? Who are you? Why are you covered in blood?" she cringed at the bodies and tried to scoot backward, but there were more bodies behind them. "What the hell is going on?"

"Mom?" Stephanie said, approaching with Danica and Penny riding her shoulder. A smile broke across

Stephanie's lips, and she raced over, falling to her knees and wrapping her arms around Hellena's neck.

"Stephie? Why are you so big? You were only ten the last time I saw you. What happened here? Are you okay?"

Finn pulled Mila in and kissed her deeply, doing his best not to get her covered in blood and green goo, but then he didn't really care.

He finally let her go, and she looked up at him. "Why is your shirt off? Are you trying to impress me?"

Finn smiled. "Are you impressed?"

"I mean, the withered arm's a little creepy, but I can work with the rest."

He frowned at the arm. "Yeah, I think I'm going to lose it. I've had another healing potion while you were gone, and it didn't do a damned thing. Guess me and Danica will be arm twins."

"I heard that," Danica called out. "You *wish* you were as young and hot as me, grandpa."

"Aren't you older than me?" Finn asked.

Danica shrugged. "Age is relative."

Finn looked at Mila, then frowned when she didn't react. "Oh, come on! I said the exact same thing and you called me a *manther*."

Mila's eyes brightened, and she smiled. "Oh, I forgot about the manther!"

"You actually forgot about that?"

"It's kinda been a busy day."

"So, if I wouldn't have said anything..."

"Totally would have forgotten all about it."

"Fuck."

# EPILOGUE

Two hours later, Finn and Mila reclined on a park bench, the blizzard still raging around them as the Huldu worked to put everything back together. Someone had found a tee-shirt for Finn to put on since he had been shredded by the Gjallarhorn. It was black, but also about three sizes too small and had a unicorn leaping across the front with rainbows shooting out of its ass. The text at the bottom said, 'me so horny.'

Mila loved it and thought it was perfect for him.

Finn had wanted to take the Gjallarhorn and keep it under lock and key, but Mila had had a better idea. She asked the Dirt Elemental if he would take it and hide it someplace no one would find it. He agreed and stuffed it into his chest before sinking into the ground, taking the horn with him.

Turned out Penny had been able to hide her magical presence, but one of the side effects of her not being able to project magic was her ability to talk had also been taken away. Finn said it was a blessing in disguise until she showed him she knew at least one phrase in sign language; two if she did it with each hand. Even Mila had laughed when they found out that the effect would last for a full week. They were fully prepared for a lot of middle fingers for the next seven days.

Stephanie and Hellena had been reunited. Preston wanted to keep an eye on her, so he had a detail assigned to follow her for the next fifty years. There were a lot of unanswered questions between mother and daughter, but it looked like Hellena's memories weren't going to come back. Finn told Stephanie sometimes it's better not to know, and just be thankful she got her back at all. Stephanie asked if she could come to visit from time to time, and Finn and Mila loved the idea. They made plans for dinner and a movie in five days. That way Penny couldn't spoil it for her.

Penny gave Finn the middle finger.

Finn leaned back on the bench, putting his arm around Mila's shoulders. He pulled her close and kissed the top of her head.

"That was insane," Mila said, staring off into the distance.

Finn nodded. "Usually is."

Mila playfully punched him in the gut. "Shut up. It is not. What do you think'll happen next?"

Finn pursed his lips. "Whatever you want, I guess. I'm game for anything."

Mila slid into his lap, a big cheesy smile on her face. "Anything?" She tapped the end of his nose.

"Sure. Why not." He shrugged. "How bad could it be?"

"You know how Danica said she got you a surprise at the mall?"

He chuckled. "Oh, yeah. I forgot all about that."

"Well, she told me what it was."

Finn raised an eyebrow. "And?"

She smiled, trying not to laugh. "Leggings."

"Leggings?"

"Yup."

Finn busted out laughing. "Okay, I'll do you one further. I'll wear said leggings out to the Refinery if you let me keep one of those." He pointed, and she followed his finger.

"You know you'll kill yourself on that, right?"

"That's what healing potions are for."

She smiled. "Fine, but you have to wear them the whole night, and it's got to be a weekend. And Danica has to be there."

"Deal." He agreed, looking greedily at the black motorcycle. "What kind of bike is that?"

Mila turned and squinted. "It's a Triumph."

Finn smiled even bigger. "That's a fitting name."

She laughed and kissed him.

He pulled back a little and looked into her eyes. "I love you."

Her face softened, and she caressed his cheek. "I love you too, manther."

He sighed in defeat.

"Fuck."


THE END

Finn and Mila have conquered the Dark Star, but their story is far from over.

Come join the gang in an all new adventure: The Lone Valkyrie series.

Six months have passed, and everyone is falling into their roles. Finn is working with the magical community to make lives better, and Mila is discovering what it means to be in the Valkyrie Sisterhood. Penny, on the other hand has a little unfinished business with Finn, concerning the promise that brought them together in the first place; her hoard.

Join Mila as she begins her life as a Valkyrie, fighting an evil she didn't even know could exist on this Terranavis in book one of The Lone Valkyrie series. Look for it shortly on Amazon and Kindle Unlimited.

Mila's story continues in *Shield Maiden*, book one of the Lone Valkyrie series from Charley Case

**Every time a shot rings out a Valkyrie earns her wings. Mila is earning hers the hard way hunting down the monsters that have taken her sister.**

It was supposed to be a simple scouting mission.

But the trail is leading her to an unexpected discovery. What if the things that go bump in the night start to slither out into the light?

**An ancient horror, full of malice and nightmares, is coming to the Idaho Wilderness.**

She should probably run, but Valkyries don't back down from a fight, no matter the risk.

Besides, there are lives at stake, and it's a Valkyries job to choose the dead. The Dwarf King would be proud.

Join Mila in *Shield Maiden* and continue the story that Finnegan started.

Available at Amazon and through Kindle Unlimited

Get sneak peeks, exclusive giveaways, behind the scenes content, and more.
PLUS you'll be notified of special **one day only fan pricing** on new releases.

Sign up today to get free stories.

CLICK HERE

or visit: https://marthacarr.com/read-free-stories/

Today I had to take one of my cats to the vet. Not to worry, it was just a routine checkup, and Alice is doing fine.

But it was a huge hassle.

I had to delay starting work by a few hours, and then when I did finally sit down to put words on the page I got a call from the vet saying that Alice was ready to be picked up. So I had to pack up my things from the coffee shop/brewery (Western Collective, hell yeah!) I had planted myself in and head across town to bring my grumpy cat home. Then once at home I had to feed her lunch while fighting off her sister and brother who had eaten when the auto feeders went off an hour before.

All fed and happy, Alice went to the couch and laid down for a nap, her day done.

My day on the other hand hadn't even started yet. I had gotten maybe 200 words down before I was called back to the vet's office. So, here I was setting up for the second time today to finally do some writing and it was already 2pm.

A day wasted.

...well, actually, it wasn't wasted. Sure, I only wrote 200 words out of the 3000 I planned on getting done, but today became about more than the writing.

While at Western Collective I struck up a conversation with a bartender/barista that I have come to know over the months I've been frequenting the place. It was a fun conversation about how life just gets faster and harder when school is over, and how they deal with the pressure. It wasn't a long conversation and to be fair it was a pretty standard subject, but in that conversation, she said something that hit a chord within me.

She mentioned something in jest along the lines of, "was it a dwarf or an elf?"

Now, what she meant was, she didn't really know the difference; anyone who reads fantasy knows the difference so well that they just wouldn't even think to ask the question. But what I heard, in my always churning brain, was "Dwarven Elf."

Or, in other words, a half dwarf half elf... what the hell would that be like? Would it be something like a thin Finn? Or would it be a short Danica? What would their abilities be like? How would the magical community react to them?

The answer to all those questions is; I have no idea, but I'm going to find out.

Maybe in this series, maybe in my War Mage Chronicles series, maybe in something completely new, I have no idea where, but the one thing I do know is that it's an idea I'll run with eventually.

After the call I went back to the vet's office and picked up my sweet girl, Alice. I started chatting with tech and she mentioned something about a cat with a bobbed tail, and my brain was like, "Okay, buddy... here we go again."

So, my closest friend Jason and his wife Nicole just lost their cat of 18 years a couple of weeks ago. Fatty Lumpkin was the sweetest little girl. All my memories of going to visit them include the little orange and white love ball we called Lump. She would come in and sleep with me for the first hour of every night, just to be sure I felt welcome in her home (anyone who owns a cat knows that the house is theirs, and they let us use the space; given that we feed them in a timely manner.).

The loss was hard for everyone, especially since we live on the opposite side of the country, and can't just go over to give our condolences properly.

Being the animal lovers they are, and missing their fallen friend, Jay and Nic went to the local shelter to "just pet some cats". The shelter attendant, trained to see weakness in those that enter the shelters doors, saw them coming a thousand miles away.

Long story short Jay and Nic are now "fostering" two fuzz-butts that came from an animal hoarders home.

These two little girls were so stressed out that one of them had an eye swollen shut, and the other, frantic to make sure her sister was safe, was fighting off anyone who came near them. An hour later at their new foster home the swelling was practically gone, and they were purring up a storm while sitting in a lap each.

Why did I think about these two while talking to the vet tech? Because both sisters have had their tails removed (we don't know why, and to be honest it's probably not worth dwelling on since they came from a hoarders home). So, when the tech mentioned a cat with a bobbed tail, I immediately thought of the sisters. Which reminded me of their names.

Goblin and Wyrm.

The names made me think "Goblin and The Wyrm", which is a pretty badass title for a story. Then I started thinking of what that story is... and let me tell you, I have a whole outline at this point, and it's pretty fucking epic. (so, look out for that one in the future)

My point in this long ramble is that I'm a writer, but that doesn't mean that my whole day is about writing. Granted, most days are just about writing; I sit at my desk of choice at 8:30am and don't get up until 4:30pm most days.

Writing is hard work.

But some days I have to go to the vet, and I get to talk to baristas and vet techs and bartenders and any number of interesting individuals who inspire me in ways they never would have imagined. I get to take those little bits of inspiration and spin them into yarns for all of you.

I could have looked at today and said, "200 words? What a failure!" Instead I looked at today as a huge success. Two great ideas in one day? That's golden!

I guess what I'm trying to say is that success is not measured by what you get done, but by what you accomplish. I got 200 words done, but I accomplished 200 words AND got two story ideas that will make my future writing all the more robust.

Don't be too hard on yourself when you feel like you've failed, instead take a step back and look at why you failed. Maybe the problem is you don't really understand the task.

I'm a writer, but my task isn't writing, it's telling stories. And now I have two more to tell.

Thank you so much for reading my book, and double thanks for getting this far. The last thing I want is for you to feel like I'm preaching at you, because I'm not; I just like to share stories about how I learned to be at peace with my crazy brain. Maybe you can feel better about yourself knowing there is someone out there just a little crazier than you ;)

Peace Fellow Humans,
Charley Case
(4:52 pm, 2/3/2020
Boise, Id)

# AUTHOR NOTES - MARTHA CARR

FEBRUARY 3, 2020

Andrew Dobell is an original with the LMBPN crew. There's a handful of us who have been here almost from the start and he's one of them. He was helping to turn out covers back when we didn't have as many people... or structure in place. And being authors, it meant we were sometimes asking for things at the last second, (hey, it wasn't just me) making changes and posting a cover and hitting publish all at once. He always comes through and his covers get noticed by readers. What more can you ask? There's also a certain calm to the guy that I appreciate. That, and his uncanny ability to draw curvy women in shiny latex for a lot of sci fi covers that sell well. I'm firmly in the realm of Urban Fantasy but I've been told that to sell a sci fi book you need some good spaceship ass on the cover. Apparently, Mr. Dobell has found a clever loophole. Really good artists are like that.

**1. What turns you on?**

I'm guessing you mean, what do I like? 12 If it's books,

that's really hard to determine, but it does have to grab me. I read all kinds of books, but mainly Sci-Fi and Fantasy. When it comes to writing, again, I like something with at least a hint of something supernatural or futuristic.

**2. What turns you off?**

The boring and the mundane mostly.

**3. Who do you most admire? Why?**

These are tough. I admire many people for many reasons. There are artists whose work I love, like Adam Hughes, and authors who's work I love, like M D Cooper and Barry Hutchison. It's hard to quantify why I love their work, but it just appeals to me.

**4. What profession other than your own would you like to attempt?**

Nothing else really. I love being a creative.

**5. What profession would you not like to do?**

Anything without any creativity.

**6. If heaven exists, what would you like to hear God say when you arrive at the pearly gates?**

I'd like a damn good explanation!

**7. What is your favorite movie?**

Ooooh. Well, again, hard to narrow that down to one. I love Blade Runner, The Dark Knight, Winter Soldier, Aliens, Tron Legacy, Ghost in the Shell, Akira, Ghost-busters, the Predator Films, T2, The Matrix... There's more, but that will do for now.

**8. Who is your favorite character and from what book by which author?**

Amanda, from my books, by me. But, other than that, I guess Motoko Kusinagi from Ghost in the Shell?

**9. What is something most people do not know about you?**

I have a bow and do a little Archery practice.

**10. What do you look forward to most in the new year?**

Creating more stuff!

**11. What's your favorite non-LMBPN series you've done?**

What's your favorite series inside LMBPN? – I guess that would be the Bethany Anne books. Having done most of the covers for them, I feel I have something of a special connection to them.

**12. Do you have a web site you'd like to promote?**

Author Site – www.andrewdobellauthor.co.uk

Cover Work Site – www.creativeedgestudios.co.uk

**If smart phones and GPS rule the world - why am I hunting a magic compass to save the planet?**

Austin Detective Maggie Parker has seen some weird things in her day, but finding a surly gnome rooting through her garage beats all.

Her world is about to be turned upside down in a frantic search for 4 Elementals.

Each one has an artifact that can keep the Earth humming along, but they need her to unite them first.

Unless the forces against her get there first.

<u>**AVAILABLE ON AMAZON AND IN KINDLE UNLIMITED!**</u>

# OTHER BOOKS IN THE TERRANAVIS UNIVERSE

The Adventures of Maggie Parker Series

The Witches of Pressler Street

Other books by Martha Carr

Other books by Charley Case

**JOIN THE TERRANAVIS UNIVERSE FACEBOOK GROUP**

**FOLLOW TERRANAVIS UNIVERSE ON FACEBOOK**

## CONNECT WITH THE AUTHORS

**Martha Carr Social**

Website:
http://www.marthacarr.com

Facebook:
https://www.facebook.com/groups/MarthaCarrFans/

https://www.facebook.com/terranavisuniverse/

**Michael Anderle Social**

Michael Anderle Social
Website:
http://www.lmbpn.com

Email List:
http://lmbpn.com/email/

Facebook
https://www.facebook.com/TheKurtherianGambitBooks/